Equinox and Other Stories

Prairiescape Books

Equinox
and
Other Stories

Short-story Fiction

by Robert Hays

Prairiescape Books
an imprint of
Herndon-Sugarman Press, Savoy, Illinois
U.S.A.

ISBN 13   978-0-9899926-8-8

ISBN 10   0-9899926-8-3

For Mr. Magnificent

Table of Contents

"There are only two or three human stories, and they go on repeating themselves as fiercely as if they never had happened before."

–Willa Cather, *O Pioneers!*

Note to Readers

This is an eclectic collection of short stories. That is, the stories are not intended to be similar in nature—all humorous, all dramatic, all light-hearted, all anything. Each story should stand tall on its own two feet, neither propped up nor threatened by another.

And yet, each story reflects in its own way human nature and the grand scheme of things in a common universe. We all are affected by the world we live in. Our surroundings may be different and the way we react to our environs individually may vary, but we play out the days of our lives in time and place. If our environment, either human or natural, is unpleasant, this is bad. If it is favorable, this is good. Whether we have but limited freedom to deal with this or wide latitude in our choices, how we choose to use it is up to each of us and it is in these differences that we find tales worth telling.

The first story in this collection, "Equinox," is a study in the universal problem of loneliness. Essie, a coal miner's widow, lives in the past. Her years with Arthur were marked by both high points and low and recollections of times long ago leave her wondering what might have been. But this is a story of triumph, brought about in large measure by action of her loving cat and long-time sole companion, Plato. Seeing beyond the darkness of a dreary winter, Essie comes to look forward to brighter days ahead.

In "The Lottery Prize," the ageing Mardel brothers might appear to be immune to the outrages of fate. Good fortune comes late in life, long after they were likely to enjoy the youthful anticipation to which it once might have led. Close on its heels comes the bitter destiny of sudden loss.

Albert's reaction is not what one might assume, but perhaps can be understood as the reflection of a lifetime of expecting little and sanguinely accepting whatever path lay before him.

Most human lives are affected by romance—attraction to another and the comfort of having that person near. "Paco's Visions" centers on the romance between Mama Jan and Captain Christien Dupuis, brought on by the most unlikely circumstances. The story also makes evident the extent to which one person's choices may play into the needs and wants of others. Could Captain Dupuis replace the lost father mourned by Paco and Rosa? And this story also manifests the opulent lifestyle of the rich alongside the modest status of those by whom they are served.

Not all true-to-life stories can be expected to be happy ones. Life doesn't work this way. People do terrible things to other people. We cannot excuse what the unnamed criminal in "An Unpastured Dragon" has done, even though we would try to understand why, and we cannot accept that he has no remorse. We can lament his troubled childhood without this affecting our view of his behavior, but can we find it within ourselves to care about the terrible tension of waiting for a jury to decide whether to let him live or sentence him to die? We can appreciate the dedication demonstrated by his attorney, Maxxi, who accepts his guilt and abhors his crimes but questions society's right to take his life. But can we appreciate her cause?

Phillips Brooks, best known for penning the traditional Christmas song, "O Little Town of Bethlehem," wrote that, "Life comes before literature, as the material always comes before the work." In other words, life *is* the material from which literature is created. Perhaps this modest collection of stories about life demonstrates the acumen of his words. ❧

"The leaves of life keep falling, one by one."

–Edward Fitzgerald,
The Rubaiyat of Omar Kayyam

EQUINOX

Trees on the south slope, which stretched away from the front of the house, were ice-coated from the cold overnight drizzle and glistened in the slanted rays of early morning sun as if decked in strands of diamonds. Essie surveyed the scene through the yellowed lace curtains of a living room window. She was grateful for the sunshine. Two weeks of gray and dreary weather had left her more despondent than usual.

Arthur had promised her brilliant winter days like this. He'd built the house on the north side of the valley after painstaking deliberation, calculating that the rewards of catching the January sun would outweigh the penalty of added heat in July and August. For insurance, he'd planted the fast-growing silver maple trees at carefully plotted locations to afford summer shade and, beyond these, the rugged catalpas in measured straight rows to line both sides of the narrow gravel lane that led up the hill from the main road. All this was a lifetime ago, and the trees were mature now—stately reminders of Arthur's intention that home should be a place of permanence.

The maple trees were among Essie's favorite heralds of spring. One day they would be gray and barren and then, virtually overnight, a delicate auburn fringe of buds commencing to burst into blossom would appear and signal a new awakening. And the catalpas called up memories of warm spring days when the children brought her bouquets—clusters of the trees' delicate white and brown flowers spilling over the edge of their water-glass vase.

Before their ornamentation by the freezing drizzle, though, Arthur's trees had stood stark and skeletal, like stick figures on a child's slate, leaving her to worry that auburn fringes and clusters of catalpa flowers still lay in the distant future.

"I'm beginning to think spring will never come," she said softly, as if speaking to herself. She actually was addressing Plato, the devoted orange tabby cat who was well into his second decade as her constant companion.

Plato rose and stretched, then surrendered the spot of sunlight on the kitchen floor where he'd been sleeping and walked toward her. Half way there, he stopped and began to bathe. Essie laughed and waved a hand at him. "Oh, go back to sleep old lazy bones," she said. "I'm sorry for disturbing you."

The living room window had become Essie's sanctuary. From here she could view the southern Illinois landscape Arthur had so loved, this land between the rivers: a giant wedge of beautiful wooded hill country bordered on the east by the Ohio and on the west by the Mississippi. And from here she could watch the changing of the seasons, the rhythmic cycles of winter dormancy and spring renewal most apparent in

Arthur's trees. The seasons afforded markers for life's passing. At times she felt as though nature's changes were the only thing she had to look forward to.

This had not always been so. On how many mornings had she stationed herself here, at this same window, and watched anxiously for Arthur's homecoming? And how many times had she felt the immense relief that came with first sight of his tired old Ford pickup, followed inevitably by a sense of guilt as she waited mute and motionless while it turned off the main road and labored up the lane toward the house? Relief because she always knew, deep down, that one day he wouldn't come home, and guilt because Arthur always wanted her not to worry, always promised that he would take care of himself so that she'd never be left to face the world alone, and always insisted that God would see him through any dangers beyond mortal control.

Essie understood that Arthur's vow of wellbeing was more from concern for her than from honest conviction. Too many times she had heard him speak with quiet reverence the names of places like Centralia or Herrin or West

Frankfort—sites of mine disasters so terrible they were permanently engraved in the lore of this region that God had either blessed or cursed with deep, rich veins of coal.

Arthur was still alive on the dining room wall, in a sober Larry Gelman photograph taken at the end of a night shift one routine day at the mine. Arthur and eight others had just emerged from the mine shaft, stepping out of the cage at the pithead and squinting in the early morning sunlight, their faces smudged with coal dust. They reminded Essie of a troupe of amateur minstrels she'd seen performing in blackface at the little theatre on the town square when she was a girl. The tragedy struck three weeks after the picture was taken.

Mr. Gelman humbly presented framed prints to Essie and a half-dozen other new widows as his lasting memorial to the lost miners. She'd heard that the photograph had become famous, published in a national magazine or some such thing, though she never knew if that was true. All this, too, was years in the past, but sometimes the pain still cut like a sharp blade, as if it were new and fresh.

Coal miners' wives learn to live with constant dread as a matter of self-survival. Essie had always known that one of the dark tunnels could become Arthur's tomb. A cave-in, or a spark and explosion, and miners' lives would be snuffed out in the blink of an eye. She had hardened herself against this possibility as best she could. But she had not prepared herself for all the finger-pointing and the uncertainties, and closure might have come quicker and more easily had it not been for the lingering questions.

The worst part was the gossip. Because no one could be sure what actually took place hundreds of feet below the surface of the earth that day when the men died, rumors had floated like dust in the wind during the weeks that followed. Blanche Griglione had viciously proclaimed the disaster Arthur's fault. She blamed him for the loss of her Paulo because Arthur had been the crew leader. Arthur surely must have led the men in the wrong direction after the initial explosion, Blanche said, so they were victims of the after-damp and helpless to escape the subsequent blasts.

Essie felt guilty because she could not

prove Blanche wrong. She wanted to fight back and not allow Arthur's good name to be smeared by Blanche's cruel indictment. Arthur was an experienced miner. His men trusted him. He never would have made that kind of mistake. But she had no evidence with which to answer the gossip Blanche had ignited.

The accusations were even more hurtful because Blanche had been Essie's best friend. From that day forward, neither had said so much as a solitary word to the other.

For her own part, Essie had lain awake night after night wondering what really happened. Only in recent years had she finally resigned herself to living the rest of her life without knowing the truth, beyond the fact that Arthur was gone.

Not that life with Arthur had been perfect. Arthur had his faults. He was human, after all, and on occasion did things for which he was sorry. Yet the shame was hers, because she always assumed that her failings as a wife had somehow brought out her husband's darker side. And she had not been left to face the world alone. There were the children: Marybeth, their firstborn, who had become the most precious treasure in Arthur's whole universe, and Daniel, man-child from the moment he drew his first breath and bedrock of strength and support for his mother at a time when there was little else to cling to. And the grandchildren. Her home had once been filled by people she loved who loved her back.

Essie—her real name was Esme, but she considered that pretentious—understood as well as anyone that her existence could have been much more difficult. She had been fortunate to have friends and family and she had been able to manage financially thanks to the union's contract with Morgan Coal Company.

But like most positives in her life, these had been severely eroded over the passing years. Arthur's life insurance money was exhausted before the children finished school and, with rising costs, the mining company's once-generous widow's pension had been barely enough to survive on for some time now.

Most of her friends and family had scattered and disappeared like dry leaves in the sweeping gales of November. Even the grandchildren were grown and gone, so that Arthur's permanent home had long since quieted from the crying and laughter and incoherent babble of innocent and sweet young voices. No sounds, no smells, no sights or touch of other humans. Plato often was the only other living being in her house for days at a time.

Essie was grateful for Roland Quidry, the letter carrier who drove his Jeep up the lane every day except Sunday and left her mail in a box fixed securely to a cedar post Arthur had set deep in the ground. Daniel had replaced the original mailbox a decade or more ago, and now the new box had rusted and the hinged lid squeaked when it was pulled open, but it was more than adequate for such meager deposits as Essie could expect.

Roland Quidry had become her principal contact with the outside world. She often sat on the shaded porch on summer days and awaited the mailman's coming. If he was on schedule, or at the very least not running too late, he'd sometimes stop and visit and express his concern for her welfare. During the cold winter months he would watch for Essie's appearance at a window then she'd wave and he would wave back and her connection with the rest of humanity would be complete for another day.

As Essie sat and thought about all the ways her life had changed, Plato brushed against her legs and gave her a stout head-butt. This most gentle of creatures wanted and expected her to notice his presence and let him know she cared that he was there, that she received and accepted his love. And feed him, of course, when he was hungry. Essie considered this a small price to pay for his companionship.

"Oh, I'm sorry, Mr. Magnificent," she said. "Your breakfast is long overdue. You're going to lose patience with me one of these days and I can't blame you."

Plato continued to rub against her legs as she stood. She might have tripped over him making her way to the cupboard, but she knew his motion and he knew hers. They had shared close space for years and learned to step almost as one as they went about the house. When Essie moved, Plato was nearly certain to move alongside.

"You're always under foot," she complained good naturedly. "One of these days I'm going to step on your tail." Even if he didn't understand her words, Essie believed, the cat recognized her moods. He was made contented by her talk. He rubbed against her legs some more and purred.

She opened a can of his favorite food and spooned half of it into his bowl. She put the rest in a plastic container which she covered carefully and placed on a top shelf in the refrigerator. After that, with Plato's immediate needs taken care of, she resumed her watch at the window.

Down near the main road, a lone coyote hurried through the frozen grass, watching carefully for any small game that might make a meal. A red-tailed hawk flew circles high above.

The sun warmed the bare limbs of the trees and the ice began to fall away, first in little nuggets and then in long, shimmering ribbons which shattered into hundreds of pieces when they hit the ground. Some of the remaining seed pods on the catalpa trees dropped with the ice. Across the valley, Essie saw a bright reflection from the metal roof of Albert Johnson's barn as it finally caught a full share of the sun's rays.

Come spring, the hills beyond the Johnson place would be blanketed with redbud and dogwood trees that bloomed beneath the canopies of the tall oaks and hickories before they came into leaf and concealed what lay below. She longed for that season, longed for the fringes to appear on Arthur's maple trees.

Essie sat and watched the interplay of sunlight and shadow until midday. She took little satisfaction in such change as she witnessed, the ice-covered world beyond her living room window no brighter once the sun had melted the ice away. The appeal of the scene before her faded with the morning hours, like a movie she'd seen too many times before. Would the bleakness of February ever run its course?

Plato was hungry again. Essie tended to his needs and fixed a sandwich for herself and made fresh coffee and sat at the small kitchen table with Plato at her feet and tried to remember other long winters. There was that one terrible January blizzard. Arthur couldn't get through the blowing and drifting snow and stayed at the mine for four days and nights while she was home with the kids and running out of food for the table. But southern Illinois winters were seldom that severe and she couldn't think of any others that were particularly hard.

"This hasn't been too bad a winter, it just seems so long," she said. Plato paid her no heed.

"If you'd been here in that blizzard you might have learned to be less particular about your food. A few table scraps would have looked pretty good."

Plato looked up at her as if he understood and if she was talking about food maybe he ought to listen. He stood and yawned and came over to where she sat and threw a shoulder into her leg and curled his tail around it the way he did when he wanted to demonstrate his comfort with their togetherness. This is what Essie supposed, anyway.

"When Arthur finally did get home, he brought in a great-big sack of potatoes and some canned goods," she went on. "He wasn't sure when he'd be able to get out again. I know, we didn't have you yet. And I'm glad you didn't have to go through that January. But I do wish you'd known Arthur. You would have liked him. Arthur was the only man I ever loved."

Much to her own surprise and to Plato's obvious puzzlement, Essie suddenly began to weep. She stemmed the flow of tears with a napkin and used it to wipe her nose. Plato watched with an air of honest concern.

"I'm all right," Essie assured him. "But you're such a sweetheart to worry. It's just that sometimes when I talk about Arthur . . ."

Plato still looked to be unsure. She leaned down and stroked the back of his head. "You wouldn't believe it to see me now," she said, "but I could have been right popular with the young men if Arthur hadn't come along when he did. I was only eighteen. Maybe I should tell you sometime about Mr. Pratt."

In truth, at the time she met Arthur Essie never had had a boyfriend, had rarely been alone with a man who wasn't family. She had been through the emotional turmoil of girlish attraction, though, first with a high school history teacher and later with a man who worked at the post office. She assumed this was love. Her fascination with the teacher went away during summer vacation. The other man, whose name was Marion

Pratt, posed a somewhat bigger challenge.

"Mr. Pratt was a good bit older than me and still lived with his mother," Essie said, choosing to go ahead and share the story with Plato now. "I'd seen him around town for years when I was a little girl and never noticed anything special about him. But one day I stopped to pick up the mail for my papa and Mr. Pratt looked at me in a way no man ever had before. It was in the spring, just after I turned sixteen."

Essie did not need to stop and think about that day before going on with her story. She remembered it well. All the way home, she had considered the expression on Mr. Pratt's face. She worried that she had blushed visibly under his gaze, but Marion Pratt had blushed too, and quickly looked away. That night before bed, she'd studied herself in the mirror, hoping to see herself the way Mr. Pratt had, and she was surprised by what she saw. She was developing into a woman. And she was pretty. Still, she might be imagining things about Mr. Pratt that weren't true. She decided to stop by the post office again tomorrow and see what happened.

"All I knew about men was what Aunt

Lornie had told me," Essie said, carrying on her one-way conversation with the cat. "Aunt Lornie loved to dress up and go dancing and it seemed like there was always lots of men who wanted to take her. My mother—Aunt Lornie was her younger sister—my mother did not approve of the way she behaved but I thought she was real cool, as the young people used to say."

Aunt Lornie had been Essie's favorite among all her blood relatives. She'd often talked to her young niece about men, telling about her own experiences, and her message in general was that men weren't much good.

"I wanted to talk to her about Mr. Pratt," Essie went on. "At least give her a hint that a man had found me attractive. But Aunt Lornie was away at the time, traveling in Florida, I think. I couldn't talk to Mama about such a thing so I was pretty much on my own."

Essie thought back to her visit to the post office after school the next day. She'd pretended to look at the patriotic posters on the bulletin board and tried to watch Mr. Pratt, busy waiting on customers at the service window, out of a corner of her eye. He was watching her, too, and though she tried hard not to she began to blush. She felt the heat creeping up her neck and into her cheeks and wanted to turn and run but Mr. Pratt finished with the last person in line and called her to the window. She stepped forward with a quarter in her hand and asked for two stamps. Mr. Pratt carefully separated two stamps from a sheet and slid them across the counter.

"Here you go," he said. "And happy equinox. It's nice to have more sunshine. Spring's here for sure."

He took her quarter and made change, counting the last pennies carefully into her hand. His finger tips touched her palm and Essie had goose bumps on her arm. She felt as if Mr. Pratt could see right through the flesh and bone that covered her brain and read her girlish thoughts. How foolish she must look. Surely Mr. Pratt would laugh.

But Marion Pratt had not laughed at her then, nor at any other time. He kept on looking at her in that way that made her feel like her blood was rushing through her veins and causing the back of her neck to tingle. Essie never mentioned her attraction to him to Aunt Lornie or anyone else. But for years to come she still had seen Mr. Pratt in a way that was unlike her view of other men.

Essie told Plato, "I stopped by the library on the way home and looked up 'equinox' in the dictionary. I'd never heard of it before. I thought Mr. Pratt must have been awful smart. I'm embarrassed to say that for a long while I made up reasons to go to the post office almost every day. And Mr. Pratt always noticed me."

It was late afternoon when Essie heard the unmistakable sound of Roland Quidry's Jeep approaching the house. She went to the window and waved when he stopped at her mailbox and he waved back and in a minute he was gone. A heavy cloud cover had obscured the sun and the day had turned dark and depressing again.

"I think the mail will have to wait," Essie said. "I doubt there's anything out there worth risking a fall on the ice for." She spoke in the general direction of Plato, sprawled on his back in his favorite living room chair sound asleep.

Essie went to the kitchen to check his

water dish. She took the dish to the sink and rinsed it clean and refilled it. She filled it too full. Water spilled as she carried it back to its usual spot at the end of the kitchen cabinets and left a wet trail across the floor. Angry with herself, she flung the dish across the room, into the sink, with a loud clatter of breaking china. Plato jumped down from his chair and ran behind a couch.

Essie clasped her hands hard against the sides of her head.

"What's wrong with me?" she said plaintively. "I'm sorry, Plato—come on out, you know I won't hurt you. I'm sorry for being so silly. I'm just not myself today."

She went to the hall closet and dug into a loose mound of linens. There had been a time when she kept the closet neatly organized, with towels and washcloths precisely arranged by color and size and carefully lined up in tidy stacks separate from the sheets and pillow cases, but she no longer bothered with such effort.

She picked the towel with the thickest pile. It had a slight musty odor, but it would be fine for cleaning up the mess she'd made.

35

Back in the kitchen, Essie got down on hands and knees and began to blot up the water. She made wide circles with the towel in hopes that she was cleaning the floor in the process. She and Plato would be the only ones to know whether the floor was scrubbed or not. She threw the towel, now wet and dirty, into a laundry basket in the bathroom.

Plato gave up his safe hiding place and approached the kitchen warily. Essie scooped him up in her arms and hugged him tightly.

"I'm sorry, kitty, you know I am," she said softly. "It's like I've been in a gray mood, like the weather. Forgive me for being an old grouch, okay? I'll make some supper and we'll both feel better."

She found a can of chicken noodle soup —the concentrated kind, that needed water to be added—poured it into a pot and let it simmer on the stove for several minutes while she got Plato's food and set a place for herself at the table. Plato had regained his composure with her stroking, and his appetite as well. He was nearly finished eating before Essie had ladled herself a bowl of soup and sat down to begin. She wasn't hungry. She ate about half the soup and dumped the rest down the drain of the kitchen sink.

The house was cold. Arthur had built it strong so that it would last, but it was not well insulated and the old furnace was not efficient. Essie got ready for bed early. She pulled an extra comforter from the closet and laid it across the foot of the bed. Plato would snuggle down beside her and help keep her warm.

As she did every night, Essie said a brief prayer as soon as she was settled under the covers. She believed in God and heaven and took comfort in the notion that Arthur awaited her in eternity. She didn't pretend to know whether they would be together in physical form, as they had been here on earth, or simply meet again in spirit, and if she asked too many questions of herself her faith was harder to sustain—especially now that she no longer went to church.

She'd once found her church to be a place of comfort, a place where her faith was strengthened and she could enjoy the companionship of friends. These friends had included Blanche Griglione. And of course there were the hypocrites— people who said the right things to Essie's face after the disaster at the mine and pretended to sympathize over the loss of Arthur but later whispered behind her back, spreading Blanche's nasty rumors. A few weeks after the tragedy she had vowed never to set foot in the church again.

Arthur had never been a religious man. Even though he professed faith that God would protect him down in the mine, he hadn't been inside a church since their wedding.

Essie prayed for her grandson Cody, serving time in a Missouri prison for making and selling something illegal. She could not remember what it was. Cody was Daniel's child and bore a striking resemblance to Arthur. He'd been only eighteen when he was sentenced to two years, and as far as Essie knew the first year had passed without incident.

Cody always had been something of an enigma. Daniel said his son simply marched to the beat of his own drummer, but Rachel, Cody's mother, was less generous. She had labeled Cody a problem child from the time he was ten years old and had pretty nearly given up on him by the time he reached his teens.

So far as Essie was concerned, she loved

all her grandchildren equally and she had been careful not to interfere. She and Arthur had raised Daniel and Marybeth to be good parents. Anyway, times had changed and who knew anymore what to expect of children? "Kids today are different," Arthur had observed many years past, "and there's just too many ways they can get in trouble." Essie always had relied on Arthur's point of view; she supposed things were even worse today.

Her thoughts were interrupted by Plato's loud snoring. She shifted her position so that he moved and the snoring stopped.

"You're even noisier to sleep with than Arthur was," she told him, and stroked his back until he was soundly asleep again.

Still worrying about Cody, she wondered how Arthur would have dealt with this troubled grandson. Arthur had been overly stern with Daniel and tolerant to a fault with Marybeth, never willing to admit to his double standard. There were times when this may have been appropriate, as Daniel was always challenging and rebellious while his older sister was a constant model of good conduct. But Essie had seen how their father's attitude was reflected in the children's behavior. She had become protective of Daniel and come to resent sharply what she saw as Arthur's outright mistreatment of their son. Arthur, she decided, would have been too hard on Cody.

Arthur's firmness had been his greatest failing, and yet it was his sturdiness Essie missed most of all—the sense that his strong arms would protect her from the terrors of the world. She missed him physically. Purposely overlooking the dreadful nights of abuse, she imagined him lying in bed at her side.

The bad nights were infrequent, after all, and not the true measure of this man. It was only when he stopped at the tavern after work, when he had too much to drink and came home angry and demanding, when he wanted things that Essie couldn't offer, it was only then that he was ugly and cruel, only on these long nights that she suffered his impossible physical ultimatums and verbal insults and cowered in the darkness concerned for her safety.

But Essie supposed all men were that way. She counted her blessings that Arthur's anger rarely had led him to strike her. Remembering the good Arthur, she finally drifted into restless sleep.

Dreams come quickly. Essie is in a pitch-black tunnel, struggling for breath in the foul air, surrounded by silence. Then Arthur is beside her. He takes her hand. "I'm a good miner," he says. "I'll lead you out." His safety lamp lights the way. There is a crosscut and to one side of it an airshaft and then they are in the sunshine and she lies on the fragrant grass and revels in the beauty of the trees and flowers and a vibrant cloudless sky. He comes to her. But it is Mr. Pratt, not Arthur, who makes love to her and comforts her and brings ease to her tense body.

She was in a deep slumber when Plato woke her, hungry and impatient. She felt as though she'd been asleep for no more than a couple of hours, but sunlight saturated the room and she knew it was late. She got out of bed and stepped into warm slippers. She trudged to the kitchen, where she fed the ravenous cat and commenced to brew herself strong coffee. It took a second serving to satisfy Plato's appetite. He curled against her feet as she sat at the table and sipped her coffee, gazing up with an expression of love and appreciation that brought the first crack to the glum mask behind which she'd begun the new day. Essie smiled and Plato purred and made apparent his contentment.

"It's just you and me, Plato, and another winter day," she said, and finished her coffee. Plato was alert, waiting for her next move. She put on a coat and told him, "We'd best get yesterday's mail. Surely the ice is all gone now."

Plato was close at her heels as she carefully stepped off the porch and made her way to the mailbox. The metal box was cold to her touch, but not frozen shut as she'd feared, and she took from it a couple of slender envelopes that obviously were not important and turned back toward the house.

Plato had wandered off to one side. In mid-stride, he suddenly stopped and sat, as if on guard.

"Come on," Essie said. "It's still too cold for you to play outside. Let's go in."

Plato didn't move.

Essie started to walk ahead, but the cat struck a familiar attitude that meant he wanted her to come. A few steps closer and she saw why. He proudly stood watch over a tiny yellow flower, barely visible among the frozen blades of grass. He looked first at the flower and then at Essie, as if eager for her to see.

She stooped low and pinched off the tender stem, separating the bloom from the frozen ground. Plato beamed with pleasure.

"Oh, my," she said, studying the delicate blossom, "the first crocus. Such a pretty little thing to come right through the cold and ice."

Plato stood and stretched, arching his back and digging first his front claws and then the back into the frozen turf. Then he rewarded her with a firm shoulder-block and stood purring at her feet.

"You just weren't going to let me miss it, were you!" she said. This was not a question, but a declaration of praise. "I've been so cross, maybe you knew how much I needed a sign of spring."

And that's what these hardy little crocuses were—a sign of spring. They were here every year, popping up as if from nowhere, perennial reminders that winter wouldn't last forever. The equinox would come. Balance. Nature's routine, the promise of long days of sunshine to warm the earth. Just like Mr. Pratt had told her.

How could she have doubted?

It wasn't the seasons that were at fault, but her own impatience. Hadn't she inhabited her little space on earth long enough to know better? Didn't spring always follow winter? And had she not learned to survive the cheerless days of January by looking forward to April?

Essie's outlook brightened. Before we know it, she thought, the maple trees will be showing their red fringe and the weigela and mock orange will be coming into bloom. And we'll be back at work in the garden.

Her senses jumped ahead. It was as if she could feel the soil, warmed by the sun and moist in her fingers, as she thinned the lily beds to make them more productive. The pink clematis on the backyard trellis had stood the coldest weather well and should bloom in profusion, and in her mind's eye she saw the waves of daisies that would transform the south slope into a sea of white. Nearer the house, the purple coneflowers and black-eyed Susans would brighten their surroundings and she could almost smell the clumps of watermelon-red monarda and hear the hum of the honeybees drawn to the succulent flowers.

Now she felt almost giddy.

"I'd like more trumpet vine on the fence," she said aloud, "and this year I think I'll try a planting of meadowsweet. Yes, I will! Who cares if it's only you and me, Mr. Magnificent? The equinox is right around the corner and we're going to be all right."

Plato rewarded her with a firm head-butt, rubbed against her legs, then led her home.

"Life admits not of delays; when pleasure can be had, it is fit to catch it."

—Samuel Johnson,
On the Life of Goldsmith

The Lottery Prize

The Mardel brothers, Albert and Wilbur, were just about inseparable. Hardly anyone in Ellisville remembered ever seeing one of them without the other. Two generations of townspeople had known and liked them and had come to think of the old fellows as more or less standard fixtures in the life of the community.

The two men looked to be the same age but Wilbur, at seventy-three, was four years Albert's senior. Wilbur was outgoing and sociable, Albert reserved by nature and polite almost to a fault. And except for each other, they were without kin. Wilbur had been married, but a sudden and virulent attack of influenza ended his Emma's life at a young age, before there were children. It took Wilbur some years to regain his spirit. Albert, so far as anyone knew, had never had a woman friend.

On days when the weather was good, the brothers sat for hours at a time on the side porch of their old Victorian house on Cedar Street and greeted passersby, friend and stranger alike. They always sat side by side on a weathered and faded old settee of indistinguishable color and pattern. Most of the grownups in Ellisville had sat with them at one time or another, discussing the weather and politics—the latter having been of consuming interest to Albert and Wilbur since at least as far back as the presidency of Harry S. Truman.

The neighborhood children also counted Albert and Wilbur as friends. Wilbur pretended to recall the Civil War. His young listeners, lacking his sense of history, did not find this astonishing. They listened in awe to his fanciful and elaborate stories about being shelled by rebels on a Union Army gunboat on the Mississippi during the siege of Vicksburg or enduring the firestorm of cannon ball and musket shot at Shiloh. Albert, one of their close neighbors often said, enjoyed Wilbur's tall tales as much as the children did.

The brothers got by on modest income. Their grandfather, a hard-driving man who built the house in which Albert and Wilbur now lived, founded the Mardel Ice and Coal Company and single-handedly shaped it into a vigorous enter-prise. The brothers' father, in turn, seemed des-tined to gain at least a modest fortune in the family business. But he had carelessly driven in front of a train at an unguarded crossing when Albert and Wilbur were teenagers. The boys worked hard to help support their widowed mother. The modern age diminished and finally extinguished any demand for their products, though, and Mardel Ice and Coal eventually went under. Now their mother, too, was long gone and the brothers lived frugally, combining their old age pensions in a single bank account.

The brothers' closeness never failed to impress those people who knew them. When Albert was hospitalized with pneumonia, Wilbur refused to leave his bedside for the first forty-eight hours. And even then, he made Doc Otto

Schramm swear an oath that Albert was out of danger. A year or so after that, Wilbur was confined to a wheelchair for some weeks after a tree-trimming accident and Albert catered to his every need. He pushed his brother around the block at least once every day, explaining that he didn't want Wilbur to feel "penned in."

"If I got real sick," Doc Schramm told his nurse, "I just hope my wife would look after me the way Albert looks after Wilbur!"

The brothers hadn't been out of town for years. They rarely backed their pristine old green Dodge sedan out of the garage except for washing and polishing. They walked the few blocks necessary to buy groceries, go to the bank or post office, or, increasingly less often in recent years, attend Sunday services at the Methodist church. This last fact was worrisome to Pastor David Becker. Pastor Becker had relied on the brothers, particularly Wilbur, for support during some of the most trying crises in his irregular relationship with the church members. Wilbur was largely responsible for the eventual congealing of the Ellisville Methodists into a unified fellowship.

Albert and Wilbur enjoyed but one simple vice: Every week, they bought a single lottery ticket. Each brother played a favored—and secret—set of numbers. They took turns buying the ticket.

"We don't expect to win," Wilbur told Lou Seiters, at whose Food King market they bought their tickets. "But wouldn't it give us something to talk about if we did!"

And one day it happened. The Mardel brothers had the great good fortune to win the $100,000 "Lucky Thursday Sweepstakes!" Word spread through town like wildfire. Everyone in Ellisville was happy and excited for Albert and Wilbur. It was almost as if the brothers' lottery prize was shared by the whole community.

Lorna Sweet, the best reporter on the staff of the *Weekly Independent*, set up an interview. Her long front-page story ran complete with a three-column picture of Albert and Wilbur, grinning self-consciously over their prize check. "It's a right smart figure," Wilbur was quoted as saying, "even after the government takes its share in taxes."

The brothers said they had talked at length about what to do with the money. Because neither of them ever had seen an ocean or been on an airplane, they'd decided to spend a bit of their winnings on a trip to Myrtle Beach. This was a place they had heard a lot about.

"We've made our reservations," Wilbur said—this is the way Lorna Sweet reported it in the *Weekly Independent*—"and our tickets are in the mail. Albert and me are pretty excited."

Lorna drew most of her quotations from Wilbur, always the more talkative of the two. But Albert said he was excited, too, and couldn't wait to see Wilbur "looking at all those pretty young women on the beach."

Lou Seiters, on seeing Lorna's article, decided that the Mardel brothers were the closest thing to celebrity the community had. They merited further recognition. He went to work organizing an event worthy of Albert's and Wilbur's new stature: a *bon voyage* party.

Lou donated food and paperware from the Food King; a half-dozen men and women who fancied themselves good cooks agreed to fix the dinner; and Sheriff Randall Gentry and his two deputies took responsibility for setting up tables and chairs in the town hall.

Lorna Sweet announced the event in another front-page story in the *Weekly Independent* and Lou Seiters had posters printed that invited everyone to come. Hardly a utility pole in town or about the surrounding countryside escaped the posters tacked up by Boy Scout Troop B. Nobody complained that the posters looked to be aimed more at advertising the Food King than the big celebration.

The weather on the day of the event proved to be exceptionally nice: sunny and mild with a gentle breeze from the west. The turnout was overwhelming. People ate and talked and enjoyed themselves, and stayed on merely to revel in the fact that two of their own had won the big lottery prize. Lou Seiters, pretending that no one else had been willing to do it, took upon himself the task of mastering ceremonies.

"There's not going to be any speeches," Lou vowed. But no one showed surprise when he rapped his knuckles on the table and, promising that his remarks would be brief, belabored in his best public-speaking voice the community's pride in the brothers Mardel. "We want to give our fortunate good friends a chance to say a few words before we leave," he said finally. "Albert, is there anything you'd like to say?"

Albert looked embarrassed. "Just to say we appreciate it," he mumbled.

"And how about you, Wilbur?" said Lou Seiters, placing his hand on Wilbur's shoulder. Wilbur, his head lowered, did not respond. Lou tried again: "Wilbur—want to say anything?"

Then Lou Seiters's face went white. "Oh, no," he whispered hoarsely, under his breath. "My dear God, I think he's dead!"

Most of those present at the celebration showed up at the Methodist church Thursday afternoon for Wilbur's funeral. Pastor Becker read from the Psalms. He tried to be upbeat, as was his habit when preaching funerals, and talked about the glories of Heaven. He described his vision of Wilbur, "clothed in robes of purple and gold and looking down upon us with that big, wide smile on his face!"

The organist played an eloquent rendition

of "Sweet Hour of Prayer." A spray of pink and white gladioli bedecked Wilbur's coffin, which sat, open, on a portable catafalque at the front of the church. Five modest floral arrangements completed the scene.

Everyone commented that it was a nice funeral. Wilbur, they said, looked very natural.

Burial took place immediately afterward in the small, overgrown church cemetery, close to a clump of elderberry bushes that grew along the fence. Pastor Becker said a final prayer over Wilbur's mortal remains. The mourners filed by Albert, one by one, offering condolences. Albert stood fence-post still and erect, his face a mask of despair.

Lou Seiters was at the end of the line, followed only by Pastor Becker.

"Albert," Lou Seiters said, "we're all very sorry. We will miss Wilbur. I know it will be very hard on you. What will you do?"

Albert hesitated. He shifted his weight from one foot to the other and then back again. "Well," he said finally, "I suppose I'll go home and start to pack my suitcase. I'm leaving in the morning for Myrtle Beach."   ❧

57

"Romance and poetry, ivy, lichens and wall-flowers need ruin to make them grow."

–Nathaniel Hawthorne,
The Marble Faun

Paco's Visions

Paco was only twelve years old, but he already knew he had a gift: He saw visions. This was something he had just discovered and he hadn't told anyone yet, not even Rosa or Mama Jan. They still believed that Marmalade, the old tortoiseshell tomcat, would come home sooner or later and he hadn't the heart to tell them what he'd seen.

It wasn't unusual for Marmalade to disappear for days on end and then show up at the back door, tired and hungry, and flaunt his independence; where he'd been was nobody's business.

But Paco knew where he'd been this time—

he'd been prowling around the swamp again and he was not coming back. The terrible vision of poor Marmalade being snatched off a log by a hungry alligator had been so vivid that Paco might have been standing on the log behind him.

Rosa would believe him if he told her about his gift, even if he did not tell her about Marmalade. Rosa understood these things. He wasn't sure about Mama Jan. Mama Jan would listen, but she wouldn't necessarily take his word the way Rosa would. He and Rosa had been through a lot more than most brothers and sisters their ages—Rosa was two years older—and had learned to trust one another completely, no questions asked.

Their lives had been much more comfortable since they came to Sanibel Island with Mama Jan nearly a year ago. That was when Mr. Sebastian hired her away from the Hotel Creole in New Orleans, where she barely eked out a living on the housekeeping staff. He gave her a generous salary and a place to live. Not just any place, but his wonderful old Sanibel mansion.

Mr. Sebastian said there always should be people in the mansion to take care of it, and it had enough room for them to live there and still leave plenty of space for him whenever he came to the island. He also let Mama Jan use the old Chrysler minivan that otherwise gathered dust in the mansion's three-car garage. Mr. Sebastian lived in Chicago and had been to Sanibel just once since they'd moved in. The only other non-family person who'd been in the house during that time was old George, the handyman Mama Jan hired when something needed fixing or there was a problem with overgrowth on the grounds. The two men who showed up regularly to mow the grass never came inside.

Paco and Rosa loved the island, but Mama Jan still missed the city. Rosa said she was lonely. She had friends in New Orleans and there had been gentlemen callers from time to time. Most of these were old men who lived in the neighborhood, seeking companionship and pleased to be seen in the company of a pretty woman like Mama Jan. They usually brought her chocolates or flowers or sometimes both.

Paco still got goose bumps just thinking about their trip from New Orleans. They had been driven to Biloxi in Mr. Sebastian's long black limousine and then rode on his yacht along the coast of the Gulf of Mexico and down the length of Florida to the island. This had proved a long and tiring trip for Mama Jan, but for Paco and Rosa it had been the most exciting thing they'd ever done. Even yet there was hardly a day they didn't talk about it.

Marmalade had been a big hit with the yacht crew. They said having a male tortoiseshell cat on a boat brought good luck.

"According to legend, he will protect us from storms and ghosts," Captain Dupuis proclaimed. "Every sailor knows that."

Mama Jan said she'd take all the luck she could get because being on the water made her nervous. In deference to her, the captain stayed close enough to shore that she never lost sight of land. Never mind that this made the trip a good bit longer, he said, and Paco could tell he wasn't being sarcastic.

Captain Dupuis's declaration had left Paco a bit concerned, though. He'd never considered the possibility of ghosts on a boat, but you always had to watch for storms on the Gulf coast and if Captain Dupuis fretted about ghosts the same as storms, maybe Paco ought to be looking out for both. But although he'd rather the captain had waited until they were close to Sanibel before mentioning either ghosts or storms, Paco had come to admire him and felt safe as long as he was driving the yacht.

Mama Jan said Captain Dupuis was very smart for a simple Cajun boatman. Paco wondered why, if the captain was Cajun, he didn't talk like one. He'd never heard the captain speak anything except proper English. Another crew member, Emile, did talk that funny way the Cajuns do and Beau, the third boatman, spoke in French now and then.

Mama Jan often pretended to hold the local New Orleans men in contempt, said they weren't fine gentlemen like Mr. Sebastian. But even young Paco could see that she had a crush on Captain Dupuis. Every time he looked in her direction she blushed like a school girl.

Captain Dupuis apparently noticed it too, and by the time they reached the island he was looking at Mama Jan most of the time.

Mama Jan invited the boatmen to stay overnight at the mansion and visit, but Captain

Dupuis said no, much as he would enjoy staying over they had to turn around and get Mr. Sebastian's yacht back to Biloxi. He said the trip back would be shorter because they wouldn't have to hug the coast like they had coming down. This embarrassed Mama Jan. She said she knew it was her fault they had to do that and she felt bad about it and she was sorry to be so much trouble. This embarrassed Captain Dupuis. He took Mama Jan's hand and pleaded with her not to feel guilty because it was his decision.

"It was my duty to make sure you had a pleasant journey," he said. "Those were Mr. Sebastian's orders. And anyway, the longer voyage gave us all more time to get acquainted. It was our pleasure."

Mama Jan blushed even deeper. Captain Dupuis held her hand for a moment and looked into her eyes. Then he and his two crewmen headed back to the yacht basin. Mama Jan and the children were left standing at the door of the mansion, waiting for the van that would bring their goods from New Orleans. This would not be an unpleasant wait; the mansion was fully furnished, the refrigerator and kitchen pantry were fully stocked, and clean beds were ready.

While they explored their new home, Paco and Rosa kept up a continuous chatter about the voyage. "Captain Dupuis is a very nice man," Rosa said. "Don't you think so, Mama Jan?"

"Fake as a three-dollar bill," Mama Jan exclaimed. "Thinks he can take a woman in with that phony charm." But Rosa looked at Paco and smiled, as if to show that she didn't find Mama Jan very convincing.

Mama Jan was not really their mother. She was their mother's cousin and their mother had turned to her for help after their father was killed in an armed robbery at the Rite Aid pharmacy where he worked stocking shelves at night. Their mother took to leaving them with Mama Jan for longer and longer periods, and then one day just never came back. Rosa claimed to remember their father, a gentle Costa Rican who'd made his way to New Orleans looking for a better life, but Paco had no recollection of ever having a father.

Mama Jan always said she liked their father very much. Paco looked a lot like him, she said, and their father would be proud of both his children. She never talked about their mother anymore. She had told them once that their grandmother on that side of the family was half Cherokee and lived somewhere in North Carolina—if she was still alive. No one ever had tried to contact her.

Life on the island had been serene. That is, until Paco had his vision. Knowing that something bad had happened even though he didn't actually witness it quickly came to impress him as an awful burden. Maybe his gift was not a gift at all. Maybe it was a curse. He wondered if God had singled him out for some special punishment.

He really needed to talk to Rosa about it, if only he could gather the courage. Rosa knew all about voodoo. She'd heard lots of stories about spells and curses and magic powers from a little Haitian friend in New Orleans and told all the stories to Paco. He didn't see much connection between voodoo and his vision, but it was clear that Rosa believed in such things.

As far as Mama Jan was concerned, Paco supposed that during all her years in New Orleans she had heard enough talk about mysticism that his gift—or curse—might not seem all that strange. Even if she didn't believe him he probably was in for nothing more than a mild scolding for his "foolish notions."

Paco hated knowing that Marmalade was not coming home. The old cat had been a household fixture for as long as he could remember. He always had taken Marmalade's presence for granted and felt a great sense of emptiness when he realized the finality of what he'd seen in his vision. No matter what, he'd never tell Rosa and Mama Jan what happened.

Mama Jan always said that having a male tortoiseshell in the house meant good luck. She said tortoiseshell tomcats were rare. She had picked out Marmalade from a litter of kittens born in the Hotel Creole maintenance room and brought him home as soon as he was old enough to take away from his mother. He'd been strictly an indoor cat as long as they'd lived in New Orleans, but once he saw his new surroundings on Sanibel he seemed to feel it was his destiny to explore the island—especially the swamp.

"I worry about that old cat," Mama Jan said one day after they'd been on the island for a few weeks. "He's a city cat and he doesn't know about the wilds of the outdoors. Too many dangers out there."

In the beginning, she went out and looked for him every time he failed to show up at the back door first thing in the morning. She eventually came to accept his tomcat ways, but she'd never become relaxed with the thought of him out there somewhere in the night.

But Mama Jan no longer worried about Paco, even when he was gone for hours at a time. Paco had promised to stay away from the swamp.

This was an easy promise to keep, because alligators are unpredictable and he was even more afraid of the snakes. Anyway the island offered enough room to roam freely without going near the swamp, including miles of white-sand beaches, and sometimes he even walked over the causeway to Captiva Island to see if he could find something different.

More than anything else, Paco was fascinated by boats. Rich tourists sailed to the island on their yachts, some almost as big as Mr. Sebastian's, and Paco never tired of watching them plough through the blue Gulf waters like magical sea dragons out for a day in the sun.

He liked boats with motors, whether they were yachts or fishing boats, and he dreamed of having his own vessel someday. Old George said he could get a job on a boat as soon as he was big enough. Paco asked how big he would have to be, but old George didn't know.

It would be nice to work for a boatman like Captain Dupuis, Paco thought. There were days when men on passing boats would remind him of the captain and Paco would dream of sitting in the stern of Mr. Sebastian's yacht and watching his hero navigate their way to a far-off destination.

Two days after his vision, Paco returned home after an afternoon spent traipsing about the island and found the mansion in turmoil. Mr. Sebastian was coming. Mama Jan was edgy; she flew about in a state of agitation, certain that a thousand things must be done. She couldn't seem to decide exactly what these were, but warned Paco and Rosa to stay out of her way.

"Go call George," she demanded of Rosa.

"The grounds have to be spruced up."

"But old George was just here last week, Mama Jan," Rosa protested. "Didn't he do everything that needed doing?"

"Who knows what he did? Just go call him, child."

"Yes, ma'am," Rosa murmured, and quickly disappeared.

"Is Mr. Sebastian coming on his boat?" Paco asked.

"Yes, he is. Why?"

"Because I'll probably get to see Captain Dupuis again."

Mama Jan pretended that this hadn't occurred to her. "Why, yes, I suppose you will," she said. Paco noticed a bit of color creeping up her neck and into her cheeks as she spoke.

"I like Captain Dupuis a lot," Paco said. "Was my father anything like him?"

"Enough about Captain Dupuis. I've got work to do. Now git."

Paco went outside and waited for George. Sitting in the shade of an ancient mahogany tree, he looked out over a mass of coral honeysuckle and passion vine to the beach and studied the sparkling blue water beyond. Only modest swells marked the serene Gulf waters. How could this placid surface ever give way to the raging force of tropical storms? But if he was going to be a sailor, like Captain Dupuis, he'd have to learn to deal with the fierce waves as well as calm seas. In his mind's eye he saw the captain at the helm of the yacht coolly facing towering waves and raging winds. His reverie was interrupted when old George arrived, nearly breathless after hurrying to the mansion in response to Rosa's call.

"What's got Mama Jan all riled up now?" George asked, scruffing Paco on top of the head.

"Mr. Sebastian's coming."

"What's she expect me to do? I done everything last week."

"I guess you'll have to ask her, George. But the last I saw she was kind of running in circles, so you may have a hard time catching her."

"Let's you and me go look."

They found Mama Jan in the kitchen, anxiously surveying the contents of drawers and cabinets as if she feared something was missing. She barely looked up at Paco and George.

"George has come, Mama Jan," Paco announced.

"So I see."

Paco looked at George, who stood waiting, hat in hand, then turned back to Mama Jan. "He was wondering what you need him for," he said. "He did his work just last week."

"I know that."

"Ma'am," George said, "did you need me to do something else, or is there things in the yard that need tending to again?"

Mama Jan finally turned from the cabinet she'd been intent on. "Mr. Sebastian's coming," she said. "We must have everything ship-shape. A month or so ago you said there was a fiddlewood tree out there someplace that needed something or other. Remember?"

"No, ma'am, I don't."

"Maybe it was one of the tamarinds, then, I don't know. Just go out there and see if you can remember what it was. It needs to be taken care of."

George nodded politely and turned to go. Paco was ready to join him.

"Wait," Mama Jan said, "Are the cabbage

74

palms all healthy? Mr. Sebastian's always concerned about his precious palm trees. Didn't something get damaged in that storm last winter?"

"No palm trees, ma'am. Maybe a couple of the little old snowberries. Anyhow, the damage don't hardly show now."

"Well, then, go on. The two of you. Just stay out of my way!"

Once safely out of Mama Jan's hearing distance, Paco and the old man roared with laughter. George clearly wasn't disappointed that there was no heavy work to do and Paco always was happy when George was free to spend time with him. George grabbed long-handled lopping shears and a rake from the gardener's shed and pretended to be cutting back the ambrosia and golden creeper that had become a bit too lush in the back yard. Paco lay sprawled on the grass.

"It ain't Mr. Sebastian's comin' that's got her all hypered up," George said. "It's that sailor—Captain Dupuis. She's sure got a yen for him."

"He's a good man."

"Never said he wasn't."

"George—?"

"Yeah, boy?"

"If Mama Jan and Captain Dupuis got married, would it be like he was my daddy?"

"If'n Mama Jan's like your mama, and I reckon she is, then I'd say it would be. Pretty much the same thing. You think he'd be a good daddy?"

"He's a good man."

"So you said. Would he be a good daddy?"

Paco hesitated. "I don't really know what a good daddy would be like," he said then. "I don't remember my daddy."

"Well, I'd say if he loved Mama Jan he'd come to love you and Rosa like you was his own, too. And if he's a good man, like you say, and he loved you like you was his own, then I 'spect he'd be a good daddy."

A broad smile lit Paco's face. He rolled over on his back and looked up at the cloudless sky. George snipped half-heartedly at a misplaced clump of gaillardia.

"George—?"

"Now what?"

"Do you believe in visions?"

"It don't matter whether I believe in them

or not. Somebody say he has a vision, he has a vision. Simple as that."

"Where do visions come from?"

"Prob'ly from way back in the head some-where, where they been layin' in wait hoping for jes' the right time and place to spring up on you."

"How come you have them?"

"I don't."

"How come anybody has them?"

"Well, my guess is that visions is the Lord's way of showin' us humans how He sees things. Jes' samples, maybe. Things you're scared of or things you're hopin' for. He lets you see what they'd be like if they happened."

"And so they might not really happen?"

"I 'spect the Lord don't know yet if they really gonna happen. He's just gettin' you ready for it. Or maybe givin' you more hope. Or may-be He's waitin' to see if you can handle it be-fore He decides if'n it's real."

"So it could be real?"

"If the Lord chooses it to be, it will be."

Paco lay silently and watched a flock of graceful ibis flying lazily overhead in the general direction of the Ding Darling wildlife refuge. The snip-snip of George's busy lopping shears drowned out the sound of Rosa's approach. She startled them both when she spoke.

"Mama Jan wants you to come in out of the heat and cool off for a while. She's got a pitcher of lemonade on the table and she said for me not to come back without you!"

Unlike many of the homes on Sanibel, Mr. Sebastian's old mansion was not on one of the inland canals that let residents tie up their boats almost right at the back door. No matter, he'd explained to Mama Jan when she first came to the island, because his yacht was too big for the canals anyway. He said that's what the yacht basin was for and his crew always put in there.

Paco regretted this. He tried to imagine what it would be like to have the yacht docked right behind the house, where he could see it again when Mr. Sebastian visited. Maybe the captain would let him sleep in one of the bunks, or maybe he could stand at the big wheel and pretend to steer the boat. Mr. Sebastian would let him do just about anything he wanted. And now

Mr. Sebastian and the captain were coming in two days and Paco's excitement kept him awake late into the night.

When he woke the next morning it was almost nine o'clock. He scrambled to get his clothes and had barely finished dressing when he heard a car stop in the mansion's circular drive-way. He rushed down the steps just as Mama Jan opened the door to two men who'd come in a shiny black Dodge with a rental company sticker on the windshield. One man was large, wearing a grey summer suit, and the other was short and slight and dressed in khaki pants and short-sleeved Hawaiian shirt.

"You're Mama Jan," the large man said as she stood aside and motioned them in. "You may remember me. I'm Charles, Mr. Sebastian's gentleman."

"Of course I remember you, Charles," Mama Jan said. "But we didn't expect you until tomorrow. Is Mr. Sebastian in the car?"

"Mr. Sebastian won't arrive on the island until tomorrow. This is Bruce, Mr. Sebastian's chef. You'll find him to be a wonderful cook!"

Bruce feigned a tip of the hat, even

though he wasn't wearing a hat. Charles looked about the living room as if seeing it for the first time. "I love this old house," he said. "Mr. Sebastian used to spend his winters here, when Miss Lenore was alive. And the three boys. We had some happy times here. But nowadays . . . well, it's just not the same."

"I'm surprised that Mr. Sebastian's taking time off to visit the island during the summer. He's such a busy man."

"He has good reason," Charles said, nudging Bruce with his elbow. "Mr. Sebastian just took a new wife. He wanted to get away from the city with his young Jennifer and have some privacy."

"Well, I'm sure we'll give him all the privacy he wants."

"But Mr. Sebastian won't be staying here. He and Jennifer will be staying in one of the condos. Bruce and I in another, where we can be of service but not intrude."

Bruce snickered and returned Charles's light-hearted elbow nudge.

"I didn't know he had a condo," Mama Jan said. "Where is it?"

"He owns two or three buildings full—probably doesn't know how many, himself. He always keeps one vacant for his own use and an adjacent one for Bruce and me. You'll still have your guests, though. Mr. Sebastian's yacht crew will be staying here at the mansion. I believe you know Captain Dupuis?"

Mama Jan blushed deeply. "I think I remember him," she said. "The Cajun man?"

"Yes, I suppose he is. But Bruce and I have to be off now. Mr. Sebastian would be put out with us if we didn't have everything ready for him and the new missus. Do you have everything you need here, Mama Jan?"

"Everything but water, I think. We have to get jugs of it. Nobody from the outside can stand our foul-tasting water, you know."

"Oh, yes," Charles said. "We have to get bottled water for cooking and drinking, as Bruce knows well."

Bruce chuckled. "You think he may want us to get bottled water for Miss Jennifer to bathe in?" he said. "We sure wouldn't want the pretty little thing made all stinky by Sanibel water!"

The two men laughed heartily. Mama Jan

shuffled her feet uncomfortably. "Sounds like you don't think too highly of the new Mrs. Sebastian," she said, not smiling.

"Aw, don't pay us any attention, ma'am," Bruce said. "It's just that, well, it's kind of funny to see a man of Mr. Sebastian's years take a wife you'd think might be his granddaughter. Meaning no disrespect."

"I believe we've said enough, Bruce," Charles said rather sternly. "We'd best get on now. I'm sure Mr. Sebastian will want to see you and the children while he's here, Mama Jan. I'll let you know, of course, before he comes."

The two men hurried back to the shiny rental car and drove away. Paco waited for Mama Jan to make the first move. She seemed unsure of herself. She pulled a facial tissue from a box on the coffee table beside her and began to twist it between her fingers, apparently unaware of her action.

"Are you worried about something, Mama Jan?" Paco asked hesitantly.

"Worried? Of course not. It's just that—well, I have so much to do. Where's Rosa?"

"I'm right here, Mama Jan."

Rosa had slipped into the room so quietly neither had heard her coming.

"What do you need me for?"

"We need . . . oh, I don't know. I seem to be at a complete loss to know what to do next."

Mama Jan sat down on the nearest chair and twisted the tissue even more vigorously. It began to fray in her hands. She seemed to notice it for the first time then, and quickly tossed it aside.

"You said we needed water," Paco advised. "Oughtn't we go to Jerry's and pick up a few jugs of it? And have we got plenty of food and stuff? Captain Dupuis and the other boatmen will be here tomorrow, Mama Jan."

"I know that, child," she said irritably.

Paco knew that when Mama Jan called either of them "child" it was time to be quiet and wait for her to say something. Rosa clearly knew this, as well, and neither of them said a word. It seemed forever before Mama Jan finally spoke again.

"Well, I guess we'd better get that water," she said at last. "I'll make a list of all the other things we might need. I'm going to be feeding three extra men—hungry men—it looks like."

Mama Jan rummaged around the kitchen for a few minutes, carefully taking account of refrigerator and freezer contents and making a cursory examination of the large walk-in pantry. She scribbled a few items on a scrap of paper and called the children. The three climbed into the minivan and set off for Jerry's, the only store on the island where the stock of groceries, meat, and produce was adequate to meet Mama Jan's demands. She said the boatmen probably would want steak and potatoes—and if they didn't they might be out of luck, because she wasn't about to try her hand at Cajun cooking.

The shopping trip turned into an hour's outing. They returned to the mansion with so many bags it took several minutes to carry them from the garage to the kitchen.

It soon became clear that Mama Jan was too preoccupied to think about dinner. Paco and Rosa made peanut butter sandwiches and poured glasses of milk for themselves. If she even noticed she gave no hint. She scurried from room to room, straightening paintings on the walls, rearranging cushions on sofas and chairs, moving books from one end table to another and then back again, disappearing up the stairs and only a moment later hurrying back down again.

"Mama Jan," Paco called, "hadn't you better stop and get some supper? You always warn us it's bad to skip a meal."

He got no answer.

"She wasn't this bad when Mr. Sebastian came before," he said to Rosa. "How come you think it's so much worse this time?"

"Oh, don't be an idiot," his sister snapped. "It's not Mr. Sebastian that has her all stirred up. It's that guy on the boat. Captain what's his name. She's been thinking about him ever since we made that trip from New Orleans. She won't admit it, I'll bet, but that's her problem."

"But how come Captain Dupuis is a problem? He's a nice guy."

"Paco, you are so ignorant! She wants to impress him big time. You know, make him notice her. It's a man/woman thing. You wouldn't understand."

Paco took a moment to let his sister's explanation sink in. Then he smiled his biggest and brightest smile. "You mean like they could get married or something," he said. "And Captain Dupuis could move in with us and be like our daddy."

"Shush. She's coming. Don't you dare let her hear you say something like that!"

Mama Jan entered at full speed, dashing to the oversized refrigerator. She hesitated, first reaching for the door and then pulling back. "I don't remember what I came in here for," she said. "What was it now?"

"Mama Jan, why don't you come over and sit with us for a while?" Rosa pleaded. "You'll wear yourself plumb out for nothing. I don't think there's anything else that has to be done."

Mama Jan didn't answer, but turned and walked slowly to the table where they sat, pulled out a chair and wearily lowered herself into it. Rosa and Paco looked at each other as if they shared a secret, but neither said anything..

"Don't you think we might put Captain Dupuis in the master suite, given that Mr. Sebastian won't be staying here?" Mama Jan asked. And, without waiting for a response, "Yes, I think we should. His two boatmen can sleep in

the room over the garage. It was meant for servant quarters, you know, or maybe it isn't right to
say 'servant' anymore—a room for the housekeeper, but now of course I'm the housekeeper,
and Mr. Sebastian brings his own chef—what's
his name, Bruce, isn't it?—but Mr. Sebastian
won't be staying here so I'll have to do the cooking for Captain Dupuis and his boatmen. My
goodness, I haven't cooked for men for such a
long time I may not remember—"

"But you are an excellent cook," Rosa interrupted. "Those men are going to eat better
than they've ever eaten before. Now stop worrying so much about it."

"Yeah," Paco added, "you haven't heard
me or Rosa complain about your cooking, have
you?"

"But what if they want that awful Cajun
stuff? I'm not at all sure—"

"How can you say that?" Rosa demanded.
"You love Cajun food. You always say it's one of
the things you miss most about New Orleans."

"Well, I don't know—just because I like it
doesn't mean I can make it good enough for a
crew of New Orleans boatmen."

"But you said they'd want steak and potatoes," Paco said.

"If they want something else they can go out and find it," Rosa declared. "How come it's your responsibility to cook for them, anyway?"

"Because—don't you think it'll be very nice to have men around the house for a few days? We want to make their stay a happy one, don't we? I mean, it's one thing to have Mr. Sebastian visit, but these are ordinary people like us. And they'll only be here for a few days . . ."

"Mama Jan," Rosa said, "why don't we all get ready for bed. You'll want to get a good night's rest, with tomorrow being such a busy day. Don't you think?"

"Well, yes, I suppose so. You children go ahead. I'll get to bed soon."

Paco and Rosa went to their rooms. They heard Mama Jan moving about the mansion as long as they were awake. She was up ahead of them in the morning, too, although this was not unusual. And instead of looking tired and drawn as she had the night before, she was radiant. She'd touched up her face with a modest application of makeup and was dressed in her brightest clothes. And to their utter astonishment she'd painted the nails on both her fingers and toes!

Paco and Rosa had barely settled down to their breakfast when Charles called. Mr. Sebastian's yacht would be arriving about noon, he said, and Captain Dupuis and his two crewmen would be getting to the mansion shortly after that. Mr. Sebastian and the new Mrs. Sebastian would pay their respects later in the week. And Mr. Sebastian wanted Charles to assure them that Paco was still his favorite little boy and Rosa his favorite little girl. He was eager to see them, and Mama Jan too, of course.

Mama Jan passed this information along and then announced abruptly, "I dreamed about Marmalade last night."

Rosa clapped her hands. "Remember what you said," she urged. "You said when somebody dreams about a tortoiseshell cat it means they're going to find love!"

"Oh, that's just silly old folklore. There's way too much of it about tortoiseshell cats. Nobody really believes those things."

Paco was surprised. "But Captain Dupuis said Marmalade brought us good luck on the boat," he said. "I think he meant it. Don't you think so, Rosa?"

"How would I know?" Rosa said sharply. "Anyway, Marmalade's not here. How's he going to bring good luck to anybody if he's run off? I wish he'd get his lazy old hide home."

Paco wanted to slide down in his chair and disappear under the table. Surely his face must show the guilt he felt at this minute. How could he explain that he was certain Marmalade wasn't coming home without telling the whole story? And how could he tell Rosa and Mama Jan what he'd seen without upsetting them terribly? In the last couple of days, every time he'd remembered his vision he'd become physically ill just thinking about the poor old tomcat being eaten by an alligator.

And last night he'd had another vision. Others might think it was a dream, but Paco knew better. As clear as if it had been taking place right before his eyes in broad daylight he'd seen Captain Dupuis standing on the dock with him and Rosa and Mama Jan, waving goodbye as Mr. Sebastian's yacht sailed away. Because he'd gone to sleep right after the vision he had not had time to consider what it meant. He'd ask George about it the next time they were together, though who knew now when that might be?

Mama Jan, apparently self-conscious about her own revelation, quickly changed the subject.

"You're good children," she said, "and I'm very proud of you. I want you both to be on your best behavior while our guests are here so they'll see you the way I do. Is that a deal?"

"Yes," Paco mumbled.

"Sure, Mama Jan," Rosa said. "It's a deal."

Paco wolfed down his scrambled eggs and toast, finished his glass of milk, excused himself, and quietly slipped out of the house. He went straight to his favorite sitting place under the mahogany tree and dropped to the ground. He could feel the warm earth through his thin cotton walking shorts and his underpants. He leaned back against the tree and gazed intently at the calm Gulf waters while struggling to sort out the confused jumble of questions rattling around in his mind.

Captain Depuis would be on the island in no time at all and Paco wanted everything to be just right. Mama Jan was nervous about the boatmen staying at the mansion and he didn't understand why. His vision of poor Marmalade being eaten by an alligator still haunted him, and now the new vision—his clear image of the captain standing on the dock and waving goodbye as Mr. Sebastian's yacht sailed away. Mama Jan had dreamed about Marmalade and Rosa said this meant Mama Jan was soon to find love. Was that real, or just silly folklore like Mama Jan said?

George said visions might be true and might not be. Marmalade had been gone long enough to support Paco's vision. But George also said a vision might be nothing more than a thing you wanted to be true and Paco wanted very much for the captain to stay on Sanibel Island, so maybe his new vision wasn't true. And even the Lord above might not know in advance whether a vision was true, George said, so how could Paco expect to know?

Suddenly, he felt a sense of relief. If even the Lord didn't know yet how his new vision might turn out, surely there was no reason for Paco to worry about it. There was nothing he could do except wait and see what happened. And hope. And keep his promise to Mama Jan that he'd be on his best behavior. That last part would be easy, too, because he wanted more than anything to be liked by Captain Depuis.

His wait was not long. Just about midmorning, Charles called and said he was on his way with Captain Dupuis and the other two crewmen from Mr. Sebastian's yacht. In less than ten minutes the shiny black Dodge pulled into the driveway and three men got out, each carrying two small pieces of luggage. Charles drove away as soon as the men were out of the car and left them planted in the driveway looking ill at ease, as if wondering what to do. Paco raced to them and grabbed Captain Dupuis's extended hand.

"Paco!" the captain exclaimed. "And such a big boy now! I think you're a foot taller than when I saw you last."

"Not that much," Paco said. "But I grew some. We've been waiting for you, Captain."

"You'll be tired of us before we're gone. Now where is Mama Jan?"

Paco didn't have to answer. Mama Jan was slowly descending the front steps of the mansion, looking straight at Captain Dupuis. She took a half-dozen steps in his direction and extended a hand demurely. "How nice to see you again, Captain," she said, in a tone of voice that puzzled Paco. It sounded as if she was addressing a perfect stranger. Had she forgotten how much she liked the captain?

"Here she is," said Captain Dupuis. "And just as pretty as ever!"

"Now don't you start trying to flatter me!" Mama Jan replied. "You could sweep a simple girl like me right off her feet."

The captain had taken her hand and still held it. The two seemed to have forgotten that anyone else was present. Paco folded his arms and waited patiently and the other two crewmen from Mr. Sebastian's yacht stood by looking sheepish, as if they felt they were intruding. Finally one of them turned to Paco: "Remember me, Paco? I'm Beau. And this is Emile," gesturing toward the third man.

"Sure I do," Paco said. "You tried to teach me to tie sailors' knots."

"And you were a good student," Beau told him. "I think we could make a sailor out of you in no time at all. Don't you agree, Emile?"

94

Paco's face brightened and Emile nodded assent. Mama Jan and the captain, meanwhile, had turned and started toward the mansion, walking slowly, she holding the captain's arm as if he was a formal escort. If they were aware of the two men and the boy coming behind, they gave no indication.

Once inside the mansion, Mama Jan directed the three men to their rooms. She told them dinner would be at six—as if it was a formal affair—and she would be serving steak and potatoes. They smiled and thanked her graciously, after which Beau and Emile headed for the quarters above the garage and Captain Dupuis went directly to the master suite on the first floor.

It seemed to Paco that Mama Jan was quite proud to be acting as hostess. If she was still nervous about the men's coming, it no longer showed.

Paco went outside and took his usual seat on the ground under the old mahogany tree. On some days he was contented to sit here for hours, just watching the boats sail by the island. He was taken by surprise when Captain Dupuis suddenly came up to him from behind.

"Do you like the water, Paco?" the captain asked.

"Yes. I want to be a sailor like you someday, Captain."

"Please, call me Christien."

"I didn't know that was your name."

"Paco, I need to ask you something. Mama Jan—does she have a man-friend?"

"You mean like a boyfriend? No, not since we left New Orleans."

"No man-friend here, then? On Sanibel?"

"No. She doesn't know hardly anybody on the island. Just old George and our teachers. Maybe somebody who works at Jerry's and people like that. She doesn't have much chance to get out."

Paco turned to look the captain in the face. The captain was smiling. This was not unusual; Paco had rarely seen him without a smile. But this smile was brighter. He thought Captain Dupuis might be the most handsome man he'd ever seen. He began again to imagine sailing a boat with the captain at the helm. And what it would be like to have him as a daddy.

"I'd like for us all to go sailing tomorrow, on Mr. Sebastian's boat," the captain said. "Rosa and you and Mama Jan. And Beau and Emile and me, of course. But I know Mama Jan gets nervous on the water. Do you think she'd like to go?"

"Yes, if you ask her. On the boat with you, she wouldn't be scared anymore."

"I'll ask her, then. If she says okay, we'll go."

Paco could hardly wait to tell Rosa. He wanted to run and find her, but he wanted even more to stay with the captain. The two sat and talked until nearly dinner time. Captain Dupuis told him how he had learned to be a sailor by working on his father's shrimp boat, how he'd once owned a shrimp boat himself, how he happened to come to work for Mr. Sebastian, wonderful stories about sailing Mr. Sebastian's big boat all over the Gulf of Mexico and the Caribbean Sea. But since Miss Lenore passed away, Mr. Sebastian didn't travel much anymore.

By the time he sat down at the dinner table, Paco was almost too nervous to eat. When would the captain ask Mama Jan about a day on the boat and how would she respond? He listened intently to the grownups' conversation. The men extolled Mama Jan's cooking, she inquired about things in New Orleans, they praised her steaks, she asked about Mr. Sebastian's health, they exclaimed over their good fortune in getting to stay at the mansion, she had questions about Jennifer.

Paco couldn't stand it any longer.

"Captain, tell Mama Jan about the boat trip tomorrow," he said loudly. "Mama Jan, Captain Dupuis says—"

"Paco, where are your manners?" Mama Jan scolded. "Please apologize to Beau. He was in the middle of something important."

Paco's face reddened. "I'm sorry, Beau," he said. "I didn't mean to interrupt."

Beau waved a hand dismissively. "Forget it, boy," he said. "I don't expect what I was saying was very important. Now what's all this you were sayin' about a boat trip?"

Everyone waited for Captain Dupuis.

"Well," the captain said, "as I told Paco earlier, I thought—with Mama Jan's agreement, of course—I thought it would be nice if we all took a trip on Mr. Sebastian's boat. It'll just sit there where it's tied up now, since Mr. Sebastian doesn't plan to go anywhere, and so I thought— well, again, it depends on what you say, Mama Jan. But I thought we might sail down to Marco Island, maybe, and have lunch ashore and come back to Sanibel in the afternoon. It'd be an easy trip, but of course if Mama Jan doesn't enjoy boating, why then it's not a good idea."

Paco waited breathlessly for Mama Jan's response. Her eyes had brightened as she listened to the captain speak, which gave him hope. He was not disappointed.

"Oh, I'd love it," she said. "I won't be a bit nervous this time, I promise. I just hadn't been on a boat before we came down from New Orleans. Now I know it's safe and all that. Yes, I'd love it. Absolutely!"

"It's settled then," the captain said. "Beau, please go check on the weather forecast while the rest of us make plans."

Beau was gone only briefly. He returned with a favorable report: "Nothing but a minor low-pressure area off the Yucatan, which should not affect us at all. I know you're conservative when it comes to the weather, Christien, but trust me on this one. We'll have a good day."

It was barely daylight when Mama Jan backed the minivan out of the garage and opened each of the sliding side doors. Rosa and Paco crawled back to the wide bench seat in the rear and buckled themselves in. Beau and Emile took the middle-row bucket seats and the captain got in front with Mama Jan.

They headed for the yacht basin and, after a brief stop at Jerry's to buy food and supplies for the galley, arrived in a matter of minutes at the slip where Mr. Sebastian's boat was docked. In no time at all they were under way, around the end of the island and heading south. The Gulf waters were remarkably calm, the surface a glistening mirror barely disturbed by an occasional ripple.

"How long will it take us to get to Marco Island?" Mama Jan asked the captain.

"Oh, with calm waters and favorable wind conditions—I'd say about three hours. We'll be there well before lunchtime."

"Too bad that old tomcat not on board,"

Emile said. "Where he at now anyway?"

"Who knows?" Mama Jan said. "Off somewhere on his own. Nobody can keep up with
that cat anymore."

Paco didn't have time to feel bad about
his vision of Marmalade being devoured by an
alligator. He was promptly pulled aside by Beau,
who said he wanted to teach the boy all about
boats. This began an intense, repetitive series of
demonstrations and definitions through which
Paco was expected to learn the meanings of
words such as tack, yaw, spar, fore and aft, jib,
head, jack lines, scuttle, keel, fathom, port and
starboard, bilge, cat head, abeam and astern, hull,
hatch . . . the list began to tax his memory as well
as his patience. Fortunately, Beau recognized
that his prize pupil was growing weary and called
an end to the session before Paco rebelled.

Meanwhile, Emile had taken Rosa to the
galley, where she helped him with lunch. When
she told Paco about it later, she made the yacht's
little kitchen sound like something out of a royal
palace except on a very small scale. And she said
Emile was her very favorite among the boatmen,
even including Captain Dupuis.

While Beau and Emile and the children pursued their own interests, Mama Jan and the captain stood in the wheelhouse and took great pleasure in one another's company. The captain showed her how to steer the boat and let her take long stints at the helm. "Just keep the coast on your left," he said, and Mama Jan enjoyed his little joke.

They sailed past Marco Island and entered Caxambas Bay. It was barely past mid-morning when they docked. The captain said he was plenty hungry, though, and if Emile had lunch ready why didn't they go ahead and eat now? No one voiced dissent. Emile and Rosa packed up the food that had kept them busy in the galley. Paco pointed out an area of clean, sparkling white sand well above the high-tide mark and that became their picnic ground.

Lunch was an elaborate spread. Platters of potato turnovers with garlic spinach stuffing, Cajun-style stuffed mushrooms, crawfish boulettes, vegetable quiche cups, and red pepper halves stuffed with spicy-sweet cheese disappeared in the blink of an eye, along with lots of sweet tea.

When he'd finished, Paco lay back in the

shade of a royal palm and wondered if he ever would want to eat again. Even the usually reserved Beau groaned aloud with satisfaction.

"I think I need to just lie down for a few hours and sleep it off," Mama Jan said. "When Emile said he'd fix a picnic lunch, who would've imagined anything like this?"

"Emile is too modest to tell you, but he was the head chef in a high-priced New Orleans restaurant," Captain Dupuis said. "And that's where Mr. Sebastian found him. Isn't that right, Emile?"

"*Oui*. And soon's we went vay-vay I know for me it's right," Emile answered. "But dôn matta now, even great chef have to pick up the dishes."

The captain laughed. "And while he's doing that, Beau," he said, "maybe you'd better go check on the weather again. I hope we don't have too much wind this afternoon."

Beau seemed barely to have had time to get aboard when he came hustling back.

"Christien," he called as he approached the picnic site, "it looks like there's some ugly weather coming. That low-pressure area that still looked real stable this morning is on the move. We'll be getting some high wind and heavy rain from the south, unless we can get ahead of it."

"Then we better get a move on," the captain said. "Hurry, everybody, scramble aboard!"

As he climbed the squat accommodation ladder, Paco experienced mixed feelings about leaving Marco Island. He would have liked to stay and explore more of this exotic place where he'd never been before, yet he was eager to get back on the boat. Beau had promised to teach him more than just words during the trip back to Sanibel. At some point, he was sure he would get to steer the yacht.

They made a fast start, with the wind at their backs. Captain Dupuis set the throttle to maximum cruise speed. The big Cummins diesel engine bellowed in response.

"We're doing a bit better than ten knots," he told Mama Jan. "In land-speed, that's close to twelve miles an hour. We won't be setting any records but it's good speed for a boat this size."

"Is that fast enough to stay in front of the storms?"

"Not likely."

Skies to the south already had started to darken. The water was beginning to get choppy, slap-slapping against the hull as the yacht hit the heightening waves. And the wind was turning, blowing as much from port now as from directly astern. The boat pitched and yawed. Captain Dupuis, speaking gently but firmly, directed Mama Jan to take Paco and Rosa below deck, "where you'll be more comfortable."

"And don't worry," he said, "there's nothing dangerous about this. Sometimes it just gets a little rough."

Going below, Paco met Beau heading for the deck. "You think I'll get to drive the boat today?" Paco asked.

"Good chance, as soon as we get through this rough weather," Beau said. "Looks now like it may get worse before it gets better, though."

Once seated in the lounge next to the galley, Paco became anxious. Although there were no portholes and he couldn't see out, the unusual motion of the boat told him the water was very rough. He could hear the wind and the splatter of rain on the deck above. Rosa slipped closer and took his hand.

"Mama Jan, do you think we might sink?" Paco asked.

"Now don't even think like that. Christien is a very good sailor. He knows what to do."

Mama Jan slipped over to the couch where Paco and Rosa sat and squeezed in between them. She put an arm around each one. "I'm not a bit scared," she said. "You don't need to be either. This little bit of a storm isn't at all dangerous, not as long as we have a good captain like Christien handling the boat. Now let's just think about what we're going to do when we get home."

She'd barely finished speaking when Beau joined them. He wore a yellow slicker and was dripping wet.

"Christien says he's going to find a sheltered cove and put in to shore. We're still somewhere south of Naples and the beach is pretty regular, but if we have to we can just anchor in shallow water and ride out the storm. Everybody all right down here?"

"Don't worry about us," Mama Jan said.

Beau excused himself and went back on deck. Emile brought glasses of ice-cold Pepsi

Cola from the galley, then returned with a tray of cheese and crackers. Mama Jan talked about mundane things. Paco knew she was trying to make him and Rosa think about things other than the storm. Much of what she said related in one way or another to Christien Dupuis.

There was a much different feel to the movement of the yacht once the captain made the turn toward the beach. Because the boat was moving parallel to the caps of the waves, the water was much less choppy. Paco no longer heard the crash of waves against the hull. The boat's forward movement stopped and Captain Dupuis and Beau joined the others below deck.

"We're at anchor, just off the beach," the captain said. "Anchor ball's up and lights all lit. There's not much of a storm out there, but the rough water doesn't make for a very enjoyable ride. You've already had enough of that."

"How long you think we'll be here?" Paco inquired.

"It looks like we probably are going to be here overnight. It will be nearly dark by the time the wind dies down and I don't like to sail at night, especially with children on board. So let's all try to make ourselves at home and get comfortable."

Emile made fresh coffee and brought out sandwiches, with chocolate milk for Paco and Rosa. The yachtsmen entertained their guests with yarns about boats and sailing. Their stories were laced with anecdotes about Mr. Sebastian and some of his funny ways, though it was clear they all held their boss in high esteem. Beau paused in mid-tale and proclaimed, "We ought to give thanks that Mr. Sebastian found us. He's as good a boss as anyone could ever ask for."

From there, each of the three men and then Mama Jan told how they'd come to know Mr. Sebastian and how he'd brought them into his "family," as he liked to call it. Her story was the best all. She brought Captain Dupuis to tears when she told about the hard times she'd endured trying to get by on the meager salary she earned at the hotel, raising Paco and Rosa as if they were her own, and how wonderful it had been for them all on Sanibel Island.

When night fell, Paco and Rosa showered and chose their bunks. Mama Jan tucked them in. One by one Captain Dupuis, Beau, and Emile bid them good night. Paco soon was fast asleep. He awoke sometime later to the sound of muffled voices. These turned out to be Christien and Mama Jan, who had gone on deck and were sitting on a hatch directly over's Paco's bunk.

"You know I have strong feelings for you, Jan," he heard the captain saying. "You're a truly beautiful woman. If there was a way I could stay on Sanibel, I'd take it in a heartbeat."

"And you know I feel the same way," Mama Jan told him. "You're kind and considerate, Christien. Paco and Rosa have come to love you, too, and I wish . . ."

This was all the conversation Paco heard. He rolled on his side and went back to sleep. There was a big smile on his face.

Charles called the mansion at one o'clock. He said Mr. Sebastian and the new Mrs. Sebastian would like to visit in the evening and pay their respects to Mama Jan and the children. "With the new wife, he's almost like a proud papa," he whispered. "And that works both ways: He's very eager for her to meet you and Paco and Rosa—especially Paco. I think he's as proud of that boy as he would be if the child were his own flesh and blood."

Mama Jan bustled around checking and re-checking every nook and cranny to make sure the house would be immaculate for her company. Christien Dupuis and his two crewmen were at the yacht basin sprucing up the boat and refueling and restocking supplies. They said it needed to be ready to go at a moment's notice, should Mr. Sebastian decide he wanted to leave the island. Paco and Rosa had gone upstairs to watch television—at least that's what Mama Jan thought.

Actually, they were talking about her. Or to be more specific, her and Christien Dupuis. Paco told Rosa what he'd overheard on the boat. Rosa pressed for more detail and Paco had to admit that he'd gone back to sleep and not heard much. Still, the two were excited enough about what Rosa called "possibilities" that they were eager for the captain to get back from the yacht basin and Mr. Sebastian and the new Mrs. Sebastian to visit.

Two hours later, when their company arrived, Paco flew to Mr. Sebastian like he was a long-lost grandfather. He'd not been eager to meet the new Mrs. Sebastian, after what he'd heard Charles and Bruce say, but when he saw her he was immediately smitten. Jennifer, he thought, surely must be the most beautiful woman in the world.

After all of the proper introductions had been made, Mama Jan took Jennifer on a tour of the mansion. The captain reported to Mr. Sebastian on the state of the yacht—ship-shape and ready to sail—and Beau and Emile paid their respects. Emile and Rosa went to the kitchen and added finishing touches to Mama Jan's dinner. Then they all sat down at the long table in the huge formal dining room and ate, chattering like family members at a reunion. When they'd finished desert—Mama Jan's homemade key lime pie—Mr. Sebastian called Captain Dupuis aside and asked if they might have a word.

As the others moved to the parlor for coffee, Mr. Sebastian stood in the middle of the room, looking like a proud papa, and asked for their attention. The room fell totally quiet.

"Captain Dupuis—Christien—and I have been discussing some very important business,"

Mr. Sebastian announced, "and we've come to an agreement. As of right now, Beau is the new yacht captain and Christien is to remain on Sanibel as overseer of my property here. This won't change anything for Mama Jan, who'll stay just where she is, but Christien will live in and watch over my other places. That's all. Let's enjoy our party."

Beau and Emile quietly disappeared. When they returned, Emile carried his worn old violin and Beau an accordion. Emile shouted, *"Laissez les bons temps rouler!"* and they began to play. The music was unadulterated Cajun, captivating, energetic, pure fun.

Mr. Sebastian grabbed Jennifer's hand and they began to dance. Christien and Mama Jan joined in. Not to be left out, Rosa seized Paco and they, too, began to swirl around the room in a dizzying circle. The old house pulsated with music and good feelings.

Most radiant of all was Mama Jan, whose smile could have lit the skies all the way to Tampa Bay. At the first break in the music, she took a handkerchief from her sleeve and began to mop the perspiration from her face. She looked to Paco like the happiest person on the face of the earth.

Mama Jan was about to speak when Paco heard a curious rattling at the back door. He ran to look. He opened the door and there on the step, dirty and bedraggled, sat Marmalade.

Paco yelled for Rosa. He scooped up the old tomcat in both arms and clutched the animal tightly to his chest. He buried his face in the matted fur, rank with the odor of swamp water, and hurried back to the parlor.

The boisterous celebration of life and love and togetherness was just getting started.

"**He** who is bent on doing evil can never want occasion."

—Publius Syrus, *Maxim 459*

An Unpastured Dragon

Of unpastured dragons the great poet wrote,
And now we understand.
Dragons that range free inhabit dark
   places, frightful, dangerous,
Perhaps devouring us with their flame.
We want them corralled, stabled, secure,
   unpastured forever
Because we are afraid.

My name would mean nothing to you. I am a monster, sub-human in the eyes of those who would pretend I don't exist. I will never again be free. And I do not care. Life is of no value to me—neither yours nor mine.

I sit and wait, in shackles and chains. The room is dreary. There are no windows, no way to see out, only a single door and it is securely locked. An attorney who is supposed to be my defender sits across the table from me and scribbles notes on a legal pad. I know that she has nothing to write; concentrating on the neatly lined yellow page gives her an excuse not to look at me.

Sitting at another table are the two armed guards—officers of the court—who accompany me everywhere I go. One is named Showalter and he's not such a bad guy. I don't know, and don't want to know, the name of the other.

They say the jury won't be out long. I've been convicted. Now it is the jury's task to say whether I live or die. Do they relish playing God? Will they go home tonight to their families and brag about how they put a fiend to death? Or will they make themselves feel good by sparing my life? For some, their decision will weigh heavily for the rest of their lives. Others will soon forget.

The attorney charged with my defense is a good person. Her name is Maxxi Rohrbach and she is from the south side of Chicago. She worked her way though college and went on to get a law degree from Southern Illinois University. She's typical of the black girls I knew in college, dedicated and serious, determined to make a difference in the world. I feel bad that she got stuck with a hopeless case like mine.

Yes, I'm an educated man. I graduated from an Ivy League institution. I'll spare my fellow alumni the embarrassment of mentioning its name. What does it matter?

Maxxi impressed me the first time I met her. "I'll do what I can to save you," she says. "But you'll play by my rules. Do I make myself clear?"

Sure, Maxxi. Very clear. No b.s.

I hadn't the heart to tell her that I didn't really care, that my life has had no meaning for as long as I can remember, that the world will be a better place without me. I'm evil. I do evil things. She deserves better—the opportunity to work with someone who deserves her help, who deserves to be saved, who has at least an outside

119

chance of being saved. I've spent enough time before the so-called bar of justice to know that she is a good lawyer. Maybe if I'd had her a long time ago . . .

But I don't spend much time regretting what might have been.

I am guilty of everything they charged me with, and much more. The only reason I didn't confess to my crimes was that I didn't want to give them the satisfaction. Had my defender let me go on the witness stand I would not have denied anything I did. What difference would it have made? The prosecutor was like all prosecutors: blood-thirsty and determined. Justice was not high on his list of priorities. A gruesome murder had been committed and his political future depended on getting a conviction.

After he showed the pictures of her body, the jurors looked at me with pure hatred. Why? The pictures merely proved that somebody had done a terrible thing, not that it was me. But I suppose they could read the coldness of my heart, the lack of concern, the fact that I felt nothing. She was dead. What did it matter?

When I was young I saw people do bad

things to other people. My world went on, unaffected. I did not feel their pain. I still don't.

If you knew some of the men I've known, you might think I looked pretty good in comparison. I would never hurt a child. I have no tolerance for those who do. There was a man named Benny in a cellblock below the one I inhabited who admitted to kidnapping, raping, and torturing two little girls. He avoided the death penalty and got two life sentences with no chance of parole because he spared their lives. I bashed Benny's head in with a barbell in the weight room. They never knew who did it. And no one cared.

I never stole money. I served time with a man who bragged about swindling scores of old people out of their life savings. He was sentenced to three years in prison and was out after eighteen months on good behavior. He never repaid any of the money. Justice? Yeah, right. Justice is a word they like to put up on the courtroom wall, in bronze letters, and pretend it's what they're all about. And sometimes it is. But most of the time the guy who stole the most money has the best lawyers and justice is nothing more than an obscene illusion.

Now Maxxi's looking at me. She says, "You okay?" There's honest concern in her voice. And in her eyes, too.

"Sure, Maxxi," I tell her. "I'm fine."

She goes back to her scribbling. Maybe she really is writing something important—like notes on her next case. I hope so. I hope she has something to look forward to, a client who deserves her. A client who actually is innocent. Not the innocence claimed by ninety percent of the miserable pseudo-humans behind bars in stinking jailhouses and penitentiaries all over the country, but true innocence. A guy, or maybe even a woman, who got caught in the wrong place at the wrong time and dragged into something they had nothing to do with. Cops want to make arrests and charge somebody, and if you just happen to be walking by and they can make a case they grab you and that's it. People like that deserve a good lawyer like Maxxi. They usually don't get one.

Showalter and Mr. Gloom share a good laugh. Showalter seems like a pleasant enough guy, maybe someone I would have liked to be friends with. Even Mr. Gloom probably would have been an improvement over most of the so-called friends I've had.

Mr. Gloom is in the middle of a joke, something about a rabbi and a nun. I can't hear him very well. "But you can call me sister," he says, and that seems to be the punch line. Showalter laughs harder. Mr. Gloom looks to be quite pleased with himself. I'm sure his joke was chauvinistic and bigoted but he wouldn't know better, or care. Men like him don't understand bigotry or racism or sexism. They have to feel superior to somebody. "Yeah, that's a good one," Showalter says.

They see me watching. The laughter ceases and is replaced by grim scowls. I refuse to look away. I continue to stare, to try to make them look me in the eye, to show some indication that they understand that I am the reason we're all here. They are uncomfortable. They look away, pretending they have paperwork on the table that needs their attention. I take satisfaction in having stared them down.

Maxxi made an eloquent plea on my behalf. She talked about humanity in general more than me in particular. Smart of her. Humanity in general may be worth saving. I'm not. I doubt that the jury bought any of it, because they understood well enough that it was me sitting before them and not humanity in general. And they'd seen those pictures. But what does it matter?

There's a chaplain who comes around to the jail every day and talks about God's judgment. What does God judge us on? Each of us is a mere collection of matter. Electrons fire and misfire in our brains and we act. We create living organisms and we destroy living organisms, both through natural impulse. I have created new human beings, little images of myself, and I have exterminated human beings. Both through natural impulse. Why is one impulse good and the other evil? What is God's formula for judging that?

The chaplain is big on redemption. To hear him tell it, it doesn't matter what you've done. Redemption is there for the taking, like picking the low-hanging fruit off a tree. I'm skeptical.

I can see that Maxxi is nervous. She stopped writing and sits quietly, tapping the eraser of her pencil on the table. She must believe that a decision is close. I look at her and she smiles. I wink, but she's already looked away, as if there was something to see elsewhere.

Showalter stands and stretches. "Get you some fresh coffee, Maxxi?" he offers. Maxxi shakes her head no. Showalter goes out and Mr. Gloom re-locks the door behind him. Do they really think I'm so foolish that I'd try to escape? Or maybe they're afraid that I have henchmen who might come and try to spring me? I'm not stupid and I don't have henchmen.

There are times when I lie awake at night and pretend that I didn't do the things I've done, that I actually am a man who deserves mercy. And I try to imagine what life would be like. But I don't spend much time on that kind of silliness; how can you visualize an existence that is totally foreign to your entire lifetime of experience? Perhaps I was innocent as a child, but I honestly don't remember ever being a child. I remember events, like my father coming home drunk and beating my mother and little sister and me, but in those recollections I don't see myself as a child. I was ten years old when my mother got enough, hid a butcher knife under her pillow, and put a stop to it. I helped her try to dispose of the body and I was happy to do it. We got caught, of course, and she went to prison for twenty years and I was sent to juvenile detention. My little sister was placed in a foster home and I never saw her again. My mother died in prison, and I never saw her again, either.

I learned a lot in juvvie. I learned to protect myself, to make sure I got in the first punch, to steal what I wanted, to trust no one. But guess what? I had become a ward of the state, and the state had an obligation to make sure I had a chance at a better life. That meant a good education. I was always smart, and I took advantage of what was offered. That's how I got to a good Ivy League college.

You don't care about any of this, and I don't blame you. What does it matter? Nothing I have told you excuses the evil things I've done. And none will matter when the jury comes in.

Speaking of which, Mr. Gloom just got back and whispered to Maxxi that there's no word yet on how close the jury may be to making a decision. Sounds like they told the judge they have some serious disagreements. They're all fools. What could be so hard? They just say yes or no, kill him now or let him die a slow death locked away in some hellhole for the rest of his days. Then they can go home and watch television and drink beer and feel proud that they've done their civic duty.

The men will be all worked up from the pictures of the naked body and the graphic descriptions they were bombarded with. They'll work it out on poor wives who will be turned off by the violent pounding they get. The jury women probably won't let their men touch them for a few months. They will feel soiled by their brush with evil, and their inherent belief that all men are animals will have been strengthened.

I wonder about Maxxi. Does she have a man in her life? Is he good to her? I like her too much to view her as a sexual being, to imagine her wanting a man to jump her gorgeous bones, or summon up an image of her flailing about in bed with some jerk who's not half the person she is.

My record may not show it, but I respect

women a great deal. My mother was a saint. I've often wondered what became of my little sister. What kind of woman did she turn out to be? The thought of some man beating her the way my father beat my mother makes my blood boil. Before my mother put an end to all that, I used to lie awake and listen to him rape her during the middle of the night. I could hear her try to muffle her screams. I wanted to kill him myself and I wish I had. Had I done so, I could feel that some good had come from my time on earth.

Showalter's coming this way. Maxxi looks up. "Wish they'd get on with it," he whispers. "I'd like to get out to a baseball game tonight."

Like I said before, Showalter seems like a pretty decent guy. I hope he makes it to that game. I never cared for baseball, myself.

We've been taught that the ancient Greeks were highly civilized. Homer wrote that the Greek soldiers took their bathtubs with them to fight the Trojan war. After a day of combat it must have felt pretty good to bathe and have their bodies massaged with olive oil.

Civilized? Yeah, right. The next day they

went back to hacking and spearing the Trojans in bloody hand-to-hand combat. As Homer put it, a Greek sword pierced a Trojan's breast and another Trojan "bit the dust." There was lots of dust-biting at the hands of those highly civilized Greeks.

Hundreds of years later, in the seventeenth century, the highly civilized Brits perfected the punishment of drawing and quartering. Drawing and quartering was a sentence meted out to criminals, especially those deemed guilty of political crimes. You couldn't cross a king and expect to get away with it.

You probably never have seen livestock slaughtered and butchered, so let me explain. Drawing and quartering consists of cutting the body open and disemboweling it, then lopping off the head and cutting the body into four pieces, or quarters. After this delicate procedure had been carried out the civilized Brits rather liked to put the head and body parts on public display as a lesson to others who might be inclined toward disloyalty.

I don't suppose anybody knows all this for sure, but from what I've read "perfecting" the art of drawing and quartering meant only partially hanging the convict first—that is, leaving him alive to enjoy the procedure.

Thinking about all this, I say to Maxxi: "Do you suppose they might find my crimes heinous enough to have me drawn and quartered?"

I don't know whether Maxxi has much of a sense of humor or not. In her business, she doesn't see a lot to laugh about. So I'm not surprised when she merely looks up at me with an expression of mild irritation and says nothing.

Across the room, Mr. Gloom and Showalter are into some serious card-playing. I hear them grumbling at each other. Mr. Gloom clearly is an impatient sort and doesn't like it when Showalter takes too much time to play his hand. Showalter apparently is accustomed to Mr. Gloom's complaints, though, and doesn't say much in response. Well, they have a pretty boring job so I can't blame them too much for not being jolly old men all the time.

But back to drawing and quartering, I've known a few cons who probably deserved it because of the horrible things they did to people.

There was a repulsive old scarecrow we called "the Pope," a murderer and rapist who loved to brag about his crimes. I heard most of his stories over and over. Sometimes he got misty eyed just remembering the pleasure he'd taken in doing the things he did. He was called the Pope because he was fascinated by the Catholic Church and traipsed around chanting sermons in Latin. He had lots of sermons. There was no point in asking him to translate, because the Pope didn't do sermons in English.

One of his victims was a middle-aged nun. He waited for her after her school let out for the day, dragged her into his car and drove to the woods, tortured her until she begged for mercy, then raped her repeatedly. Then he slashed her throat. He wanted a keepsake or two, so he cut out her vagina and slashed off a breast and carried them around in his coat pocket for a couple of days.

"She was so beautiful," he would say, "and she gave me so much pleasure that I just couldn't let her go."

He used vulgar language, of course, but I won't. Like I said, I'm an educated man.

Sorry for rambling. I was talking about civilized people. That would include us Americans, right? But how many innocent men, women, and children did we leave buried under all the rubble left from our "shock and awe" attack on Baghdad? Easier, I suppose, when you can just lob in missiles from long distance.

Now here's my point. Like I said, I don't care about anybody's life, neither yours nor mine. But I hate hypocrisy. Civilized folks will have no qualms about putting me to death, even though they don't really know for sure that I deserve it because I wouldn't give them the satisfaction of confessing.

Do you know how many innocent men— maybe a woman or two, even—have been put to death? Nobody does. Nobody denies it happens. Too bad we didn't have DNA a long time ago

Maxxi's watching me closely now. She says, "I don't think it will be too much longer. You doing okay?"

"Sure," I say. "Sitting here in your good company beats the hell out of time in my room back home."

Maxxi looks a bit puzzled for an instant. Then she gets my meaning, that "home" is a filthy jail cell I've occupied for the duration of the trail. She pretends to laugh.

Mr. Gloom and Showalter seem to have grown tired of whatever card game they've been playing. Showalter heads over our way. I can see what's coming. He flirts with Maxxi, never realizing what an old fool he looks like when he does that. I mean, Maxxi is a gorgeous young woman, ten times smarter than he is, too. What in hell could he have that would interest her? But he doesn't seem to know that and she's much too classy to blow him off the way she should.

"You worked many cases with this judge before?" Showalter says.

"This is my third," she tells him.

"Slow as molasses in January, ain't he?"

"I guess I'd just say he's thorough. He doesn't let anything get past him."

Showalter obviously doesn't know crap about the law, nor courtroom procedures, nor the way judges operate. He just wants to hit on Maxxi. He switches to another subject: "George and me have played about all the two-handed pinochle we can stand for one day. You play?"

I assume "George" is Mr. Gloom.

"Sorry," Maxxi says, "I've never cared much for card games."

"I'd figured maybe you was a bridge play-er," Showalter says. He's not going down with-out a fight. He edges closer. His body odor is rancid and powerful.

Maxxi tells him, "As I said, I've never cared much for card games."

"You reckon this jury's gonna be out much longer?"

"You never know about juries."

"Bet you read them pretty good, though."

"Trying to read a jury can be a dangerous game."

I try not to laugh. Maxxi's not playing along. I can see that Showalter is becoming a lit-tle uncertain of himself. But he regroups and takes another stab at it. (Sorry, poor choice of words. Stabbing isn't something I should be talk-ing about, I suppose. But what does it matter?)

He says, "Young woman like you couldn't have been at this all that long."

Uh, oh. I guess I don't know much about

women, but I know she's not going to take that comment well. And she doesn't.

"Mr. Showalter," Maxxi says coolly, "I'm not inclined to talk about my professional background in front of my client. Now if you don't mind—"

"Excuse me, ma'am," Showalter exclaims. "I'll go on about my business."

I can't tell if he's angry or hurt or embarrassed or what. I can see that he knows he's been bested, though, and I don't think he'll try to get close to Maxxi again. I want to give her a high-five or something. I want her to at least look up so that we can make eye contact. I want her to see how proud of her I am. But she doesn't look up. She goes back to her legal pad, the long yellow sheet with the thin blue lines on it, and starts scribbling again. Damn, I hate that pad!

But like Maxxi says, you never know what to expect from a jury. I have had a bit of experience at this. If you believe you have one figured out and think you know what it's going to do, you are most likely in for a surprise.

A jury up in Washington state that looked

at me with pure contempt through the whole trial took half an hour to come back with a "not guilty" verdict. I was guilty as hell. And the prosecutor, a careful old lawyer who'd surely worked more than his fair share of cases, did a solid job of proving I was. I walked out of that courtroom laughing in his face, although I'd actually kind of admired the way he ripped my lawyer to shreds. But like I said, you never know about a jury.

Even though I beat that one, I did spend a year as a guest of the Washington taxpayers. They run a pretty good system. The main thing I remember from that experience is Chief Redskin. He was a Chehalis Indian and quite possibly the smartest con I ever came across. He hated being called Chief Redskin, which no doubt is the reason his friends and neighbors in the institution persisted in doing it. I never was sure what he was serving time for. I doubt that it was anything violent; he wasn't the violent type. He was a slight man of indeterminate age who always spoke in a soft voice.

Chief Redskin was the only man I ever served time with who could hold his own with me in discussions of philosophy, religion, and literature. And he was way ahead of me when it came to science.

He was the one who explained the concept of dark matter to me in a way I could understand. But I'm not going to try to explain it to you. You probably don't care. You can't see dark matter. Sorry if I underestimate you.

Science never has been my strong suit, though. I'd rather talk about literature. I know the classics. I've read them. And I can tell you something about the classics professors in the elite universities, like the one I went to. They surround themselves with the literature of an earlier age and get lost in it. Most of them have no clue about what goes on in the real world of today.

Years ago there was a classics professor at one of the Midwestern schools who was a hot-shot leader in the John Birch Society, if you remember that illustrious organization. He got in trouble for a big convention speech in which he talked about a "beatific vision" in which he woke one day and found that all the Jews had evaporated from the face of the earth. I'll bet that went over real big with the Jewish alumni. I suppose most of the Birchers are long gone now.

There's a world of good books besides the classics, too, and I'll have lots of time to read, regardless of what the jury comes in with. A man can be on Death Row for a long time.

Beau Geste is one of the most compelling novels I've ever read, and you probably never heard of it. It's the kind of book you find in prison libraries. Never anything new. Only old books that have been there for years, worn and dirty, because there's no longer funding for new books. If you know of any organization that gets books to prisoners please help it out. There are a lot of guys who, unlike me, deserve that kind of help.

One thing that's usually available to cons is the Bible. Some actually do find comfort in it, I believe. A lot of them pretend to, and pretend that they've gone through some kind of conversion that they claim has made them better men. That seems to carry weight with parole boards and that's reason enough for them to make the claim.

I'm not here to judge, though. There's a line in a Shakespeare play, "Julius Caesar," maybe: "Take each man's censure, but reserve thy judgment." Old Will was a wise man.

I glance at Maxxi and catch her looking at me. She sees that she's caught my eye.

"I think it's good they're taking so long to reach a decision," she says.

I smile. But I'm thinking, What the hell? How long could it take to figure out that I don't count, that it doesn't make any difference what they decide? Just come to some conclusion and get it over with. Get on home to your bitchy wives and wasted husbands and screaming kids and barking dogs and be done with it.

What does it matter?

"The really blood-thirsty juries usually don't take long," she says, then catches herself. "We can't get our hopes up, of course. Juries are unpredictable."

I say, "You gave them something to think about."

Maxxi knows I mean this as a high compliment. She looks pleased. I wonder if she could possibly understand how little I care. There is no quick way out in this system. They may give me the needle, but it won't happen soon. I will just waste away in a cramped hole in the wall on Death Row, maybe for years. That would be marginally better than life, I suppose, but I won't be celebrating the decision whatever way it goes. Still, it would be good for Maxxi to get credit for winning. She deserves it.

Across the room, I can see that Showalter is still smarting from his brush-off. He's mumbling something to Mr. Gloom, holding a hand in front of his mouth to make sure Maxxi can't hear him. Mr. Gloom nods knowingly. Showalter reddens as he speaks. She got his dander up, no question about that. She hasn't looked over that way, and I'm glad. I think she's pretty much oblivious to their presence as long as they leave her alone.

Whatever Showalter's problem is, I don't think it has anything to do with the fact that Maxxi's black. He's not the smartest man on the planet but I don't read him as racist. Most likely he just can't accept being put down by a female.

I remember vividly the instant I first saw Maxxi. One of the jail goons came and got me, said I had an important visitor. I don't get many visitors, important or otherwise. The goon didn't know who she was. I did. My new defense lawyer was due, a volunteer from the National Coalition to Abolish the Death Penalty—an organization of do-gooders determined to save me from the needle. Not just me, of course, but every murderer and rapist and other heinous crime committer facing capital punishment.

Maxxi wasn't what I expected. She was genuine. And she laid it on the line, right from the get-go.

"Just to make clear where I'm coming from," she told me, "I won't waste one minute of time trying to make you look like anything but the contemptible creature you are. If I'd been on the jury, I'd have led the charge to convict you. I'm here for one reason. We don't believe a civilized state should be in the business of putting people to death. Period. If I can, I'll save you from a death sentence. That's my job and I'll do my best."

If I am not completely accurate in repeating her words I apologize, but I know I have the substance of her statement right. And this sums up my relationship with Maxxi very well. She despises me, but she wants to save me. Go figure.

I didn't expect much from her in the beginning. I've seen too many of these "dedicated" lawyers who have no clue. But I found out pretty quickly that Maxxi was different. I couldn't con her, and neither could anyone else. She's way too smart. She had studied my case and she knew I was guilty as sin, which means she knew I'm not worth saving. She'll do her best to save me, though, because she believes in a principle. That's Maxxi.

Even as I scribble this—writing in handcuffs is not easy—I sense her concern. I feel her eyes on me. Those clear, intense eyes, so darkly beautiful. She cares. It's not about me, it's about the principle. It's about who gets to play God. Hubris. Mere mortals assuming powers that are supposed to be reserved for a deity. But what difference does it make? And who am I to worry about such things? I've taken lives and I feel no remorse. Maxxi's a better person than I.

My mother was a better person, too. She was courageous, like Maxxi. A 120-pound woman who has the guts to take on a 220-pound man who had abused her one time too many. A woman should never have to fight off a man.

The woman I did those things to wasn't courageous. She was a narcissist—thought she was important. No one is important. When I was ten years old I received an A on a class paper and my mother said A's make a student important. I showed the paper to my father and told him it meant I was important. He said, "Yeah, so just go stick your finger in a glass of water and see how big a hole you leave when you pull it out." I didn't have to think about it very long to understand what he meant.

Maybe the woman I did those bad things to had a right to her own opinion about herself, even if it was wrong. I didn't know her. Was there anything about her I could have admired, the way I admired my mother and the way I admire Maxxi? I don't know. I suppose I never gave her a chance. That wasn't fair. I'm sorry for that. If I have any regret it is for that, not being fair. Yes, I took her life, but what does it matter? A life is meaningless. My life is meaningless. Your life is meaningless. And the woman I did those things to . . .

But my mother, and Maxxi—maybe their lives mattered. Maybe I've not been fair. Maybe if I had a little more time, had another chance, maybe things could have turned out differently. But what is done is done. But you don't care about any of this and I don't blame you. Why should you?

Showalter and Mr. Gloom are stirring. They apparently have heard something. Maxxi looks at me. There is no discernible expression on her face.

The jury is back. Soon we'll know what they decided.

I'm sorry, Maxxi.

But what does it matter?

༺༻

"As writers become more numerous, it is natural for readers to become more indolent."

–Oliver Goldsmith, *The Bee*

About the Author

Robert Hays has been a newspaper reporter, public relations writer, magazine editor, political campaign manager, and university professor and administrator. A native of Illinois and a U.S. Army veteran, he holds three degrees from Southern Illinois University. He taught in Texas and Missouri and retired in 2008 after a long journalism teaching career at the University of Illinois. He has spent a great deal of time in South Carolina, the home state of his wife, Mary, and was a member of the South Carolina Writers Workshop. His publications include a diverse array of academic journal and popular periodical

articles and ten books, including his collabora-
tive work with General Oscar Koch, *G-2: Intelligence for Patton*, and one published in paperback
edition under a different title. Two of his four
novels were nominated for the prestigious Push-
cart Prize literary award. Robert and Mary make
their home in Champaign, Illinois. They have
two sons and a grandson and for a dozen wonderful years were blessed by the presence of an
extraordinarily intelligent and handsome orange
tabby cat named Eddie. As readers may surmise,
Eddie was the inspiration for Essie's Plato in
"Equinox."

This slim volume is offered as a modest
memorial to Eddie. And, yes, that's Eddie on the
cover.   ❧

Other Books
by Robert Hays

Fiction

Blood on the Roses
The Baby River Angel
The Life and Death of Lizzie Morris
Circles in the Water
Early Stories from the Land (editor)

Non-fiction

Patton's Oracle
Editorializing 'the Indian Problem'
A Race at Bay
State Science in Illinois
G-2: Intelligence for Patton
        (with Gen. Oscar Koch)
Country Editor